"What I do with my leading ladies
is acting. I'm not acting right now.
What I'm thinking and feeling is all real."

She shifted in her seat. "I don't believe you."

"Then believe this."

He lowered his head and pressed his lips against hers
with enough firmness to let her know he was serious but
light enough for her to pull away if she didn't want the
kiss. Her body shook, and her lips parted with a gasp.
He wasn't a man to pass up an opportunity, and took the
chance to deepen the kiss.

He never believed in electricity or sparks igniting when
a man kissed a woman, but something he'd never felt
before happened as he kissed her. His skin tingled, the
blood rushed through his veins, his senses heightened to
everything around them. The sweet scent of her perfume,
the softness of her lips, the way she tasted of champagne,
all seemed amplified. And like a man who'd gotten a taste
of something he really liked, he dove in for more.

He put his own glass down on the tray and brought his
hand up to feel the softness of her hair. She made a sexy
whimpering noise before her own hands came up to
clutch his arms.

Dear Reader,

Ever watch your favorite celebrity in a movie or
television show and wonder how it would be to hang
out with them? Well, that was the what-if question that
sparked my idea for *A New York Kind of Love*. And since
I write romance, I used my favorite British actor as the
inspiration for the romantic hero in the story.

My heroine, Faith Logan, has spent so much time taking
care of others that she deserves a romantic Hollywood
ending. Once Irvin Freeman felt the sparks between
himself and Faith, he had to be the man who gave her
the world.

I had so much fun writing Faith and Irvin's
happily-ever-after. I hope you enjoy reading their
story. I'd love to hear your thoughts via Facebook
(facebook.com/synithiarwilliams), Twitter (@SynithiaW)
or shoot me an email at synithiaw@gmail.com.

Sincerely,

Synithia W.

A NEW YORK KIND OF Love

SYNITHIA WILLIAMS

HARLEQUIN® KIMANI™ ROMANCE

Recycling programs
for this product may
not exist in your area.

ISBN-13: 978-0-373-86436-2

A New York Kind of Love

HARLEQUIN®

™ www.Harlequin.com

Printed in U.S.A.

Synithia Williams has been an avid romance novel lover since picking up her first at the age of thirteen. It was only natural that she would begin penning her own romances soon after—much to the chagrin of her high school math teachers. She's a native of South Carolina and now writes romances as hot as their southern settings. Outside of writing she works on water quality and sustainability issues for local government. She's married to her own personal hero and they have two sons who've convinced her that professional wrestling and superheroes are supreme entertainment. When she isn't working, writing or being a wife and mother, she's usually bingeing on TV series, playing around on social media or planning her next girls' night out with friends. You can learn more about Synithia by visiting her website, synithiawilliams.com, where she blogs about writing, life and relationships.

Books by Synithia Williams

Harlequin Kimani Romance

A New York Kind of Love

Visit the Author Profile page at Harlequin.com for more titles.

For my aunt, Annie Mae "Duke."
I miss you.

Acknowledgments

Many thanks to Sharon Cooper for pointing out
a certain pitch contest that resulted in the publishing
of this book. Thank you to Danita, my blurb whisperer,
for always answering my frantic emails when I need
quick feedback. Also, thanks to Tia Kelly for the
virtual support as I wondered if this story would
see the light of day. And, as always,
many thanks to my fantastic husband, Eric.
Your support of my writing career makes every book possible.

Chapter 1

"Congratulations, Faith Logan. You're the lucky winner of a weekend in New York with Irvin Freeman!"

Faith jerked her cell phone away from her face, frowning at the unfamiliar number on the screen. This had to be a joke. Her eyes darted to the two other nurses sitting around the nurses' station. Neither appeared to be concealing a smile. There were no covert glances her way to see if they'd duped her with some elaborate prank. She looked up and down the hall, but as usual for a Wednesday in Laurel County, South Carolina, the labor-and-delivery ward of the hospital wasn't very busy. Only one mother who'd had a baby earlier that day was walking down the hall. Dorothy, the older nurse, even stood and left the station to check on the mother, instead of sticking around to hear if Faith fell for the joke.

She put the phone back to her ear. "Excuse me?"

"You heard correctly," said the overly bright voice

on the other end. "You won the grand prize in the contest held by Starting Over, Irvin Freeman's foundation to raise alcohol awareness. Out of the thousands of entries accompanying donations to the foundation, your name was drawn. You are the lucky woman chosen to spend a fabulous, all-expenses-paid weekend in New York City with Irvin Freeman. Your prize includes a makeover, and you will be Irvin's date for the premiere of his new movie, *Running from Murder*!"

The woman's voice rose with each word until she sounded like a speaker on the stage at a "gee, life is great" high school prom.

"Is this a joke? I'm at work, and I really don't have time for jokes."

There was a pause before the voice continued in its prom-queen tone. "This is no joke, Ms. Logan. Don't you remember entering online?"

Faith frowned and tried to remember entering a contest. All her money went to her parents' medical bills and household expenses. She didn't have extra money to donate to the foundation or extra time to enter a contest.

Except for that one time…

She spun around to glare at the nurse closest to her. Marie, her best friend since she'd moved home two years ago and the person who'd helped her land the job at Laurel County Hospital, flipped through a magazine. Faith nudged Marie with her foot. When Marie looked up, she nailed her with a "this is your fault" look. She'd known it was a bad idea when Marie urged her to enter. At the time it had seemed like a good idea to contribute a few dollars to a worthy cause. Never in a gazillion years had she expected her name to be chosen.

Marie held out her hands. "What's wrong?"

Instead of answering Marie, Faith responded to the

woman on the phone. "Yeah, I remember entering that contest. I just didn't expect to win. What weekend is that? I don't even know if I can go to New York."

Marie's dark eyes widened, and she jumped from the chair to bounce on the balls of her feet next to Faith. Even without her Tweety Bird scrubs, Marie would look like a woman far younger than her thirty-three years. Her pixie cut and always-smiling features in a dark brown heart-shaped face made her instantly likable.

"Can't go?" The voice lost some of its peppiness. "Ms. Logan, this is the opportunity of a lifetime. You will be the envy of all women. A five-star hotel near Times Square…"

Faith tuned out as the caller went through all of the reasons—some of them valid—why she should go. Excitement tickled her insides, and she felt the urge to bounce around like Marie. But the cold, hard reality of her life tamped it down. Reality had smacked her in the face when she'd given up her fantastic job, lost what she'd thought was the guy she'd one day marry and moved from Houston back home to take care of her parents.

She wasn't bitter—that particular emotion was a drain on energy she couldn't afford to waste. She'd give it all up again if she had to. But going out of town right now was out of the question. Her mind raced with all the reasons this wouldn't work: Who would watch her parents while she was gone? What if it was a weekend she was scheduled to work? All of her leave was used up from taking her mama to doctors' appointments. What would she wear? Her "new" clothes were two years old and were the complete opposite of stylish or trendy. Unless scrub chic suddenly became the fashion rage.

Then there was the biggest reason not to go. Irvin Freeman: dark eyes, mahogany skin and a swagger that would put Shaft to shame, topped off with a British accent. The man oozed sex with every breath he took, and he probably expected the winner of this thing to fall into a gooey puddle of estrogen at his feet.

"I appreciate the offer." Faith cut in on the prom queen's stream of reasons why she should be falling over herself to get to New York. "But I'm not sure—"

Marie snatched the phone out of Faith's hand. "Hello, this is Marie, Faith's, um, personal assistant. We'll do some maneuvering with her schedule and make sure she's there."

Faith tried to grab the phone back, but Marie skipped away to the other side of the nurses' station. "What weekend is it, again?" Marie nodded at whatever the caller said and flipped to the calendar with the work schedule. "Perfect! She's available for that weekend. You have her email address from the entry form, correct? Just send the details and copy me, and I'll get her to the airport on time."

Marie rattled off her email address and said a few more words. When she hung up the phone, she squealed as if she'd won the prize herself. The screech got the attention of the other nurse and the mother walking down the hall.

"You are the luckiest woman alive!" Marie rushed over and gave Faith a hug, surrounding her with exuberance and the smell of her strawberry body spray.

"That depends on your definition of *lucky*. Marie, I can't go."

Marie leaned back and gave her a hand wave that said "Whatever." "Oh, yes, you can. And you will. Even if I have to knock you out and drive you to New York myself. Girl, you just won a date with Irvin Freeman. How are you not excited about this?"

Dorothy and the mother walking in the hall quickly

caught on and chanted their agreement. Faith visualized a weekend listening to Irvin brag about how great it was to be him. Sure, he always appeared down-to-earth and approachable in television interviews, but a man who had half the women in the world drooling over him couldn't be that centered. All his apparent humbleness probably hid a mountain of arrogance.

"My parents," Faith said, not wanting to get into what would surely be a debate with Marie if she dissed her friend's favorite actor. "Who's going to help them?"

"They'll be okay for one weekend. I'll look in on them personally every day you're gone."

"Do I work that weekend?" Faith crossed the station and picked up the schedule book.

"No, you're off."

Faith dropped the book and crossed her arms. "If I'm off, you're working. You won't be able to check on them."

Dorothy came over to stand before Faith, looking just like the surrogate grandmother she was to every baby born on the floor. "Your mom is doing so much better than she was when you first came home. If you prepare meals before you leave, she can heat them up for herself and your dad. Don't forget, you're not in a large city anymore. Your friends and neighbors are happy to help out."

Dorothy was right, but Faith had done everything for her parents on her own. It was her way of making up for not being there when the bottom fell out of their lives. She wasn't used to accepting help from neighbors. Besides, doing so would only increase her regret. The thought tightened the knot of guilt that had made its home in her gut since she got the call that her mama was unconscious in the hospital after suffering a stroke.

"I don't want to be a burden," she said.

"Burden, shmurden," Marie said. "You won't be. You

going on this trip will be the highlight of the year for half of Laurel County. The newspaper will probably do a write-up about you before and after. Do you know how many people will be happy to say they helped out while you went away for an all-expenses-paid weekend with a Hollywood movie star?"

Faith did chuckle at that, because it was true. Nothing this exciting had happened since Tamara Blake from Laurel High School won Ms. Laurel County and was first runner-up in the Ms. Patriot pageant back in 2001. People still bragged about their part in her win, from selling her a pair of earrings to bringing over fried chicken the night the family had a watch party.

"I get that," Faith said, "but I just don't feel right asking other people to look after my parents. And this thing is just a few weekends away. I don't have anything to wear to something like that."

"You get a thousand dollars of spending money. Buy what you need while you're there."

"A thousand dollars in New York is probably like five dollars here. It won't go far," Faith said.

"If it'll buy you a sexy dress that'll make it impossible for Irvin Freeman to keep his eyes off you, that's far enough."

Faith couldn't help but visualize the eyes referred to on a recent list as "most likely to send a woman into cardiac arrest." The guy did have a way of looking at his leading ladies with such heat you could practically hear the sizzle on-screen. To think he would turn them on her was laughable. Yet her heart did do a disloyal skip against her ribs.

"The man dates models and Oscar winners," Faith said. "Even if I were naked, he wouldn't be interested."

"Every man is interested in a naked woman," Dorothy said, laughing. Marie nodded. The idea of being naked in front of Irvin only increased Faith's body heat.

Nope. Stop. Don't go there.

Even if she were to travel to New York—which she really doubted she could—she wouldn't be sleeping with Irvin Freeman. She loved the guy's movies and thought he was a great actor, but in his charming TV interviews, there were always questions about his love life. He was constantly linked with his frequent costar Selena Jones and photographed with a string of other actresses and models between his on-screen hookups with Selena. Faith would be setting herself up to look like America's biggest fool if she went to the city with even the slightest intention of landing in bed with him. He'd laugh at her attempts, or worse, take her up on it, and she'd be the latest groupie with her name attached to his. Something she'd never live down here in Laurel County. She couldn't afford that, not with all the work she'd done to keep the Logan name free of scandal over the past two years.

A more chilling thought crept across her mind. Going on this weekend trip would put her in the spotlight even if she wasn't attached to Irvin for more than a few days. People might want to know more about her. Which could lead to questions about her family—and her twin. She wanted to go on pretending her twin had magically disappeared into thin air.

"I won't be naked with Irvin Freeman. I won't be anything, because I'm not going. They can pick another name. I have too much to do here."

"Stop it," Marie said. "You don't have too much to do, and you aren't a horrible daughter if you take one weekend to enjoy yourself. It's been two years. Go and have a great time. Your parents would agree with me."

"I know they will, because I'm going to call them now and tell them the good news," Dorothy said, picking up the phone.

"Dorothy, no. Don't bother them," Faith said. Her mama had been urging her to do something fun for the past month. If she got wind of this, she'd knock Faith out and lend Marie her wheelchair to roll Faith to the airport.

"Too late. It's ringing. Get ready to pack your bags, girlie, because you're going," Dorothy said. "Hey, Virginia, guess what? Your daughter just won the trip of a lifetime."

Marie did a little dance. Dorothy grinned and gave her a thumbs-up. Faith's palms sweated. This was not a good thing. Fate had a way of hitting her in the gut when she least expected it. And once again, it was ready to give her a sucker punch.

Chapter 2

"Well, she could have sounded a bit more enthusiastic."

Irvin looked up from the script he was reading. Kitty Brown, the head of his publicity team, stood staring at her cell phone. He'd barely heard her over the various conversations of the members of his *entourage*. A word that made him cringe inwardly—and at times outwardly—whenever he said it. The entourage was Kitty's idea; he would be perfectly fine without the lot of them. It was days like this he missed the anonymity that came with being a poor kid from the dodgy end of London. Now, thanks to Kitty, all his appearances were preplanned and scheduled for potential photo ops.

"What's wrong, Kitty? She didn't scream until her voice gave out before breaking down in tears?" He was only partly teasing. He still couldn't get over the dramatics some women went through when they met him.

"What screaming? The woman didn't scream, sigh, cry or show the least bit of gratitude that her name was selected."

Kitty crossed his crowded living room, the night sky and twinkling lights of the New York skyline visible behind her through the wall of windows in his flat. Her jet-black hair had one bright red streak in the front, which stood out against her sienna skin and the all-black suit she wore.

"Hopefully, she'll be more excited once it sinks in what she's won. I can't have the winner of your first charity contest frowning in every picture."

"How do you know she'll be frowning?" Irvin asked, glancing at his watch. It had been ten hours since the entourage had arrived to prepare for his appearance on *The Tonight Show* that afternoon and decided to stick around afterward. He was ready for all of them to leave and give him a moment of peace.

"I can hear frowns," Kitty said, waving her hand. "This woman was frowning."

"I don't care if she smiles or not," Irvin said. "I did this to raise money for the foundation. The money we raised will do a hell of a lot more than having the winner smile in your photographs."

"True, but I expected more. I didn't make you the country's most desired man only to get some lackluster response."

"I'd prefer a lackluster response every now and then."

"Don't tease," Kitty said. "You'd be bored without all this." She held out her arms to encompass the ten other people milling around the flat, each one either talking on the phone or making connections via social media. All in an effort to keep his name in front of people and build his image.

Some days—days like today, actually—he wanted to tell the lot of them to sod off. But he couldn't deny that being Hollywood's biggest celebrity had its perks, the best one being the money. Money brought safety and security. Two things he'd gone without for most of his childhood. And the money kept rolling in with every action film or dramatic role he churned out. Telling Kitty to bugger off wasn't worth losing the security blanket his celebrity afforded.

He must be tired, or he wouldn't be so annoyed with his normal routine. The New York premiere and contest weekend would be the end of a whirlwind of promotions and premieres for the film.

"Bored, maybe," he said, "but I wouldn't regret a slight decrease in all of the attention that comes with being a celebrity."

"No one likes a hermit, Irvin. You're approachable, which makes America love you all the more. Stuck-up celebrities aren't bankable."

He'd argue that some celebrities who shied away from the limelight were, but his mobile phone chimed. His heart rate revved up like the sports car he'd driven in his last film, as it had done every time the phone rang since the day he'd sent his screenplay to Kevin Lipinski a week ago. Kevin was one of the most sought-after and successful producers out there. Every film he touched turned to box-office gold, and if he liked Irvin's screenplay and agreed to produce the film, he might be Irvin's ticket out of the camera's glare and right behind it. Irvin wanted to direct.

The mobile's chime indicated a new email, which sent anticipation and dread flowing through his bloodstream. There were only two answers he could get.

Kevin would either love it or hate it. Both answers scared him.

He pressed the email icon on the phone and held his breath. Then released it in a sigh of disappointment. The new message was a party invitation. He unsuccessfully tried to tamp down his frustration. How long did it take to look at a script?

Kitty rambled on in the background about plans for the premiere. A member of the entourage let out a loud laugh at whatever the person on the phone with him had said. And another flipped the channels on his sixty-inch television with the volume turned up to high. It was information and annoyance overload. Irvin was done.

"Now that you've informed the lucky winner, we can call it a day," he said, cutting off Kitty's speech. He held up the script he'd been trying to read ever since they got back. "I've got to get through this." Another action movie. Not bad, really, but he knew the drill. The formula for his success didn't change much: he'd save a beautiful young woman, run through traffic in a big city with no shirt and haul around a big gun.

"No, we can't call it a day," Kitty said in a rush. "We need to go over the itinerary. Every moment of the premiere weekend has to be planned perfectly."

"Something that you can do without my direct input. Just tell me where to go and when to be there. The only thing I care about is when we present the check to the head of the foundation. Make sure there is plenty of time before and afterward for me to talk with him and the staff. I want to know if there is anything they need me to do to help the cause."

Alcohol awareness wasn't the sexiest issue for a celebrity to pick up. Kitty thought he should be kissing kids in third-world countries or building playgrounds for at-risk youth, where the photo ops were. He did contribute some to those causes, but preventing and stopping alcohol abuse were his passions. He'd witnessed the damages of alcohol abuse firsthand.

"Now I'd like my flat back," he said, looking at the people buzzing around. He used his normal charming tone of voice, but there was no mistaking the underlying steel beneath.

Kitty huffed but didn't argue. She was good at reading when he was tired of the show.

"Fine, but at least go over the itinerary before the end of the week." She grabbed her bag and pulled out a thick folder, which she handed over to him. "It took a while, but I managed to dig up a picture of the winner."

He flipped open the folder to find the photo. A woman with thick, dark hair and clear reddish-brown skin, wearing a conservative navy suit, stared back. Her lips were curved in a cool smile that didn't reach her eyes. Kitty should have known better than to expect this woman to scream. She didn't look the type. He frowned and studied her professional demeanor; he wouldn't have expected her even to enter the contest.

"Where did you get this picture?"

"She used to be the chief nursing officer at East Houston Regional Medical Center. It was her employee ID photo."

"She's no longer there?"

"No, left two years ago. Something about an illness in the family. I couldn't dig up a more current picture. Can you believe she doesn't have a profile anywhere?" Kitty said it as if the idea of going without an online presence was akin to going without electricity.

"Some people prefer their privacy." He looked away

from the picture to eye Kitty. "If she's not online, how did you dig this up?"

"I can't have you going out with a person with a rap sheet, Irvin, really. Before we called and confirmed her as the winner, I did some digging."

He glanced at the pinned-together woman in the picture. He doubted she would appreciate the probe into her life before being confirmed as the winner. He smirked. Well, she'd better get used to it. She'd be a pseudo celebrity while spending the weekend with him. Still, he felt a pang of regret for the digging, no matter how necessary it might have been.

"If you've got enough information to know she's not a criminal, no more researching into her past."

"For now," she said. She turned to the group. "Okay, people, let's get out of Irvin's way."

The lot of them packed up their phones, tablets and other gadgets. With waves, well wishes and another reminder from Kitty to review the itinerary, they were gone. He relished the silence for a few minutes. It seemed like a hundred years since he'd had an entire day of silence. He couldn't imagine a day in the future when he would.

"Full mouths shouldn't complain," he could hear his mother saying. It had been her way of telling him to shut up whenever he tried to say something about the beating she would take for stealing money from his dad just to put food on the table.

He pushed the uncomfortable memories aside. His mouth was full. If the lack of quiet or personal time was a side effect, then he wouldn't complain. His mother had endured far worse. She might not be around to enjoy the perks of his celebrity anymore, but childhood lessons died hard.

He flipped through the script and found the standard love scene. It had a full back shot. Kitty would love that. If she had her way, her number one client would go shirtless in every scene and have at least one back shot in every movie. It made her job of promoting him so much easier.

He tossed down the script in disgust. *Full mouth. Full mouth. Don't complain.*

Still, he checked his phone and silently hoped for a call from Kevin about his script.

There was a knock on the door. If it was Kitty returning to tell him another thing for the premiere weekend, he would lose his mind.

He checked the peephole, relaxed and opened the door with a smile. "What on earth are you doing here?"

Dante Wilson, the R & B star with a fan base as big as Irvin's, grinned from the other side. "I've got time before my concert tour and decided to come early for your promotional weekend."

Irvin shook his head and stepped back so his friend could walk in. "Why do you need to be here for my weekend?"

"Kitty thought it would be good to show off your high-profile connections as you become the highlight of this woman's life," Dante said. "Her words, not mine. Jacobe is coming up from Florida."

"Brilliant. I haven't seen Jacobe in weeks," Irvin said.

Jacobe Jenkins was the starting center for the Jacksonville Gators. The twenty-eight-year-old had been drafted at the end of his freshman year of college, let the easy money and women go to his head and started his professional basketball career as a wild party boy. Irvin and Dante had met him about a year ago at a party and become mentors for the young man. He still partied, but he wasn't getting into any foolish trouble anymore.

"But you didn't have to come early."

"It wasn't just for you. I met this model who's doing a show here this week."

That made more sense to Irvin. "Can I get you a drink?"

"You know you can." Dante shut the door behind him. "You drinking?"

Irvin shook his head. "I've had my one for the day."

"Kitty didn't push you to have two?"

Irvin laughed. "Kitty always tempts me to have two. But two leads to three and…"

He went to the bar to fix a whiskey for Dante and a cola for himself.

Dante crossed the living area to stare out over the skyline. The living definition of a pretty boy, he looked younger than his thirty-two years in designer jeans, white shirt and tie with a gray vest. Whereas Irvin was growing weary with the celebrity life, it was all Dante knew. He was the son of music legends, had grown up in front of the camera and enjoyed the fame that came with being a star.

"You should sell me this apartment," Dante said when Irvin came over and handed him his drink.

"You shouldn't get your hopes up," Irvin said and took a sip of the cola.

"One day I'll convince you."

"I doubt it."

Dante chuckled and lifted the glass. "Are you going to bring her here?"

"Who?"

"The winner of the contest." Dante gave him a sly

look. "Are you going to show her all that New York has to offer?"

"You know I don't bring women back here. It's the one place where I can escape, when Kitty's not around, at least." They both chuckled at that. "Besides, I doubt I'll get a half hour alone with the woman. Kitty will have every appearance scheduled and I'll just show up, do my charming smile, sign an autograph and then come back here to blessed silence."

"Pity."

"Not at all. This isn't a sleazy way to shag some woman. I can go for a ride without going through this much trouble. It's to raise money for the foundation."

"I'm just saying it wouldn't hurt to have a little fun out of it. Obviously if she entered, she's interested in you."

"I'm not taking advantage of a fan just to get my kicks. Besides, I have more important things to worry about than showing her a good time."

As if summoned, his phone chimed again. He rushed across the room to where he'd left it on the bar. Disappointment stooped his shoulders as he read the email from Kitty, reminding him to check the itinerary. With a swear, he dropped the phone back onto the bar.

"What's got you so worked up?" Dante asked.

"I'm waiting on a response about my screenplay."

"You finally sent it off. Good for you. You know it'll get picked up."

"I don't want it picked up because of who I am. I want it picked up because it's a good story."

"Who cares why it's picked up as long as it is? You worked on it for over a year. Push your weight around in Hollywood and get it made."

"That's not the way."

"It is the way. What's the point of all this fame if we don't put it to good use?" Dante spread his arms to encompass the spacious area.

"I'll wait and hear before I make a decision about pushing my weight around."

"Who did you send it to?"

"Kevin Lipinski."

Dante cringed. "He's the toughest producer out there. And he hates screenplays from superstars. Are you trying to kill your writing career before it starts?"

"If he says yes, then I'll know it's good. If he says no…he'll at least give me a reason why he doesn't like it."

"And tear you to pieces in the meantime. There's nothing that guy likes better than to put celebrities with inflated egos in their place."

Which was exactly why Irvin had sent it to him. If he had any chance of getting behind the camera, this was the test. If Kevin liked his script, Irvin planned to barter and plead to direct it. He'd earned his money and his fame, repaid his mother the debt he owed before she passed away, and now he was ready to move behind the camera. He loved Hollywood, loved the satisfaction of bringing a story to life and the pride when it was done well. But he could experience all those things without being the half-naked guy on-screen. It was his one shot to keep the security he had now without many of the headaches.

"I don't have an inflated ego to burst," Irvin said.

"You say that now, but wait until his comments come back."

Irvin drank his cola to swallow the sinking feeling that Dante might be right.

Chapter 3

"I don't have to go," Faith said, twisting a pair of underwear in her hands.

Virginia Logan rolled her wheelchair across the threshold into Faith's room. She shot Faith the same "are you crazy" look she'd given her when Faith was a girl and asked to stay out past her curfew. Except now the left side of her scowl drooped a little. It was still a vast improvement from the complete loss of motion and feeling Virginia had had on that side right after the stroke.

"Have you lost your mind, child?" Virginia asked in the softly slurred voice that still held a lot of her old spunk. "You deserve this vacation and a dozen more like it."

Faith tossed the underwear in the bag. "I don't deserve anything. I should stay. I could have filled in for one of the nurses who needed off this weekend. I'm so close to paying off the credit card, it seems foolish to lose twenty-four hours of overtime to hang out with an actor and party."

"There's nothing wrong with enjoying yourself when the opportunity arises." Her mama wheeled closer and reached out her hand. Faith took it and squeezed. "You gave up a lot moving back here from Houston to take care of me and your dad. As much as I hate that you had to sacrifice so much, I'm also grateful."

"It was nothing. Especially after what Love did to you two."

Virginia sighed and let go of Faith's hand. "It's time for you to stop feeling guilty over what your sister did."

"I know, Mama, but we're twins. I should have sensed that she was capable of taking advantage of you."

Virginia laughed and patted Faith's arm. "This is real life, not some sci-fi movie. Just because you're her twin doesn't mean you can read her mind. There was no way any of us would have sensed that Love would get caught up in drugs or steal our money and skip town while I was in the hospital."

"But shouldn't I have realized that something was wrong with her? Heard it in her voice, or had some clue that she could be so heartless?"

"Your sister isn't heartless, Faith. She's sick. Thank the good Lord she finally agreed to go to rehab."

Faith turned away from her mama. She walked over to the closet and calmly took down a few sundresses for the trip. She wanted to scream at her mama's insistence on trying to find the good in Love. Despite years of dealing with Love's fight against addiction, when she'd wiped out their parents' savings the day after her mama suffered a stroke, Faith considered that the end of her relationship with her sister. Her parents had worked hard to build up their nest egg for retirement. Her mama had worked as a schoolteacher and principal for twenty years. Her dad had been a superintendent at a delivery company for years until he was flung from his delivery truck four years ago in an accident and broke his back in three places. Thankfully he could walk, but the injury prevented him from working. Her mama had taken care of him before her stroke.

Faith couldn't forgive Love for stealing from their parents. Who were already struggling after her dad's injury. From what her mama said, Love had got away with all of their savings. Savings that would have gone a long way toward helping pay the ongoing medical bills and retrofit the house to accommodate her disabled parents. All things she'd depleted her savings to pay for and worked hard to continue to pay for.

"Love isn't sick, Mama. She's a junkie," she said, not bothering to hide the contempt in her voice. She walked back to her suitcase and tossed the dresses inside.

Virginia took out the dresses and started folding each of them. "Don't hate your sister."

"After what she did, it's hard not to."

"Family is family, and she'll always be your sister. I know it's hard for you to understand how she let drugs take over her life, but she wants to get better." Virginia placed the folded dresses in the suitcase. Then she gave Faith a direct stare. "And when she's out, we'll do what we can to help her. Right?"

Faith looked away to zip her bag. That was a promise she couldn't make. This wasn't Love's first stint in rehab. She'd believed her sister once before, and less than a year later, her sister had betrayed their parents.

"If you're not going to talk me out of going, then I guess I'd better go catch that plane," Faith said instead.

Virginia sighed but didn't push.

Faith took her overnight bag from the bed. "I've made dinners for every night and they're in the freezer," she said.

Virginia shook her head and chuckled. "I know, Faith."

"And Marie said she'll check in on both of you every day. I'll keep my cell phone with me the entire time. If anything happens—"

"Nothing is going to happen, and there isn't much you can do from New York anyway," Virginia said.

"You're right. I should stay."

"Child, come on and quit fussing. Everything will be fine." Virginia turned her wheelchair around and left the room.

Faith followed her mama to the front of the house. It had taken most of the past two years to retrofit the house with wider doorways, bathroom handrails and other changes to make life easier for her parents. After Love's grand theft, Faith had offered to move her parents to Houston, where she had the salary to take better care of them, but they'd refused. They'd both lived in Laurel County all their lives and didn't want to move. If they insisted on staying, then Faith insisted on making sure their house was worth staying in.

At the front of the house, they went out into morning air, already warm and humid for early June. Marie sat on a white porch rocker, talking with Faith's dad. Jimmy Logan and Marie were both laughing, probably at a joke that Marie had made. Her friend was always good at making her parents laugh.

"Well, I guess I'm set," Faith said.

The smile on Marie's face fell. "You're going wearing that?"

Faith ran a hand across the sleeveless lavender top

and jean shorts. "What's wrong with my outfit?" Faith asked. "I'm going to be on a plane all morning."

"And when you get off, you're meeting *Irvin Freeman*. I knew I should have come over and picked out your outfit."

Jimmy placed his hands on the walker in front of him and stood. "She looks beautiful just as she is." He shuffled over to her. "You have a good time up there. Don't worry a bit, and take dozens of pictures for me and your mom, okay?"

She smiled and leaned over to give him a hug. "I will, Daddy."

"Let's get you to the airport," Marie said.

"Did I tell you where the spare key is?" she asked Marie. "And don't forget that I called in my daddy's prescription and it'll be ready later today. I left the money—"

"On the kitchen table," Marie cut in, rolling her eyes. "I know. You've told me and your parents a dozen times. Just go and have fun and quit worrying about things here."

"But I just want to make sure—"

Marie took her arm and pulled her toward the steps. "We got it. Wave goodbye to your parents."

Faith couldn't wave because she had to grab her bag as Marie dragged her by her other arm down the porch. Her parents waved and grinned as if they enjoyed watching Marie pull her away.

"Call me if you need something," she said to them.

"You just have a great time, child," her mama called back.

Her parents looked so happy for her, she thought as Marie drove off. She'd have to try to enjoy herself for their sake, at least. Truthfully, a small part of her was excited about going to New York and not having to worry about how much an item cost or how much the meal was before ordering it. She missed that part of her old life, but she didn't reflect on it too often. She'd done what she had to do, and there was no need to relive memories of a past that wasn't coming back.

As they pulled away, she couldn't help but take in the wheelchair ramp that needed replacing and the patch on the porch roof that leaked during hard storms. There was still so much to do, so much to fix. Since Love had robbed them blind, fate had kicked in to make sure everything that could go wrong did, including the house. She should stay at home, tending to those items, not travel to New York to party. No telling what bad luck fate had in store for her for going on this trip.

Hours later, Faith rolled her overnight bag off the plane, into LaGuardia Airport. She moved with the crowd toward the exit, anticipation and nervousness making her hands slick on the handle. She'd traveled around the South and West a lot, but she'd never been to New York. Even though she hated leaving her parents, this trip was giving her the opportunity to see the city, something she wouldn't have ever done on her own.

On the plane ride, she'd convinced herself to find the silver lining in winning the contest. Since she'd got the call that her mama had had a stroke and arrived to find out that her sister had stolen all of their money, she didn't put a lot of trust in luck.

But she refused to become one of those angry, bitter women who couldn't appreciate things. Since her family had practically pushed her out the door to come, she would make an effort to enjoy herself and the city. She even admitted that it might be slightly cool to meet

Irvin Freeman. However, she doubted the star wanted to spend the entire weekend playing tour guide. She could definitely suppress any eye rolls or sarcastic remarks if he did turn out to be a stuck-up snob during the few limited interactions she was likely to have with him.

She hoped.

She found her way to the pickup area of the airport. The instructions she'd been given said a car would be waiting for her. She only hoped she could find it in all of the activity.

A cameraman, a photographer and a guy holding a large sign with her name on it were the first people she saw. No problem recognizing her ride.

A woman with a bright red streak in her black hair stood next to the sign guy. She was dressed in a black suit that hugged her body so closely it had to have been custom-made for her. She fired off directions to the men. She must be the one in charge.

"Hi, I'm Faith Logan," Faith said, walking over to the group that was getting the attention of everyone in the departure area. "I guess you're my ride."

The woman in the suit stopped talking and spun to face her. The smile on her face flickered for a second, about the same amount of time it took to do a quick inventory of Faith's hair and outfit, before she got her features back in order. Faith wasn't sure what that was about, but this woman probably made her living sizing people up in one look.

"Faith Logan, welcome and congratulations! I'm Kitty Brown, Irvin's publicist and your host for this weekend," she said in the cheerful voice Faith recognized from the phone call.

The photographer lifted his camera and pointed it in Faith's direction. Kitty shook her head and motioned

with a finger for him to lower it. "Not now. We'll get
a shot of her meeting Irvin instead of coming off the
plane." She turned to Faith with another big smile. "And
we'll get you just right for the introduction."

"I really don't need anything extra just to meet him,"
Faith said, not liking the implication that she was somehow not ready to see the guy. Granted, she had hoped to
put on a little makeup—lip gloss and some mascara—
and even change into one of her dresses. But the way
Kitty came across, it was as if Faith hadn't spent the
past few hours on a plane with an hour layover thanks
to engine problems.

"Nothing extra," Kitty said, "but we can…freshen
you up a bit. We don't have a lot of time. Your plane was
delayed, you know." Kitty said it as if Faith had some
part in that. "So instead of the elaborate wardrobe, hair
and makeup session we planned, we can go with a few
changes for the photo shoot. We'll save the major makeover for before the club tonight."

"If the photo shoot is me meeting him for the first
time, why do I need to change clothes?"

Kitty stopped in the middle of turning to the rest of
the crew to raise her eyebrow at Faith. "Well, we can't
shoot you in that outfit."

Faith bet that eyebrow and disdainful tone made people quake, but she had worked for one of the meanest
hospital administrators in Houston. She'd been raised
in the South, where an older woman could throw shade
so fast and easy you wouldn't realize she'd called you a
bitch until two weeks later. Kitty didn't intimidate her.

"What's wrong with my outfit? Look, I'm willing
to go with the flow, but I will not be insulted. Not my
clothes, hair or anything else. If you wanted a starlet

type, you probably could have picked one, but you didn't. You chose me. So you're getting me."

The corner of Kitty's mouth rose in a cynical smile. "A random-number generator chose you, not me. But I know how to make do with what I'm given. The offer wasn't given as an insult—it's part of the weekend. Makeover and photo shoot with Irvin. Don't you remember that in the itinerary?"

"I haven't read the itinerary," she admitted.

Something very close to relief came across Kitty's face. "No wonder you aren't very enthusiastic. Just wait until you hear about all the fun I have in store for you. Prepare to be pleasantly surprised."

Kitty slid her arm through Faith's, as if they were old friends, and headed for the door. With a wave of her hand she indicated that the rest of the crew should follow, before diving headfirst into a speech on how lucky Faith was.

Faith tried to summon up the small amount of enthusiasm she'd felt on the plane, but Kitty barely gave her a chance to think, much less absorb it all. Plus, the woman wouldn't take a breather so Faith could call her parents and let them know she'd arrived. It was unlikely that anything catastrophic had happened since that morning, but she would have felt better checking in. However, as Kitty kept up the chatter out to the limo and on the ride to the city, Faith gave up hope of calling until they reached their destination. She couldn't help wondering if Kitty's constant chatter was her punishment for going on this trip.

Chapter 4

Irvin flipped through the pages of the latest *Men's Health* magazine as he lounged on a sofa in the Manhattan studio of photographer Rafael Sims. Kitty was late, which was very unusual for her, but he wasn't in a rush. The photo shoot with him and the winner should take about an hour, and his only afternoon plans were to not check his emails every six minutes. He wasn't doing too well with that. Rafael had helped distract him for a few minutes with idle conversation until the photographer had got a call. Irvin glanced at his watch; five minutes had passed since he'd last looked. Which meant he might as well check his phone again.

He put down the magazine and picked up his mobile. As expected, there were no emails from Kevin Lipinski. He would have been better served leaving his mobile at home. He tossed it back onto the glass table in front of him and picked up the magazine.

"Is there anything I can get you while you wait?" Rafael's young assistant came over and asked. Her smile indicated she offered a lot more than water or juice. She'd checked on him every five minutes since he'd arrived. He knew, because it was how often he'd checked his mobile.

He gave her a smile but shook his head. "No, thank you, Tina. I'm fine."

"I don't mean to be a bother. I just know that I hate waiting. Sometimes it helps to have a distraction," she said, emphasizing the last word.

Inwardly he groaned. If he wasn't *the* Irvin Freeman and was just a plain bloke walking down the street, would she even give him a passing glance? He doubted it. When he was growing up, his looks were considered average at best. Amazing how swagger, money and fame had taken him from regular guy to sex symbol.

He held up the magazine. "I have a distraction," he said, not letting the smile drop from his face. He might get annoyed with the groupies, but he was never rude. Full mouths couldn't complain, after all.

"Oh, well, if you need anything, just call me."

She turned to walk away, and he did watch her stride across the room. She was beautiful—he'd give her that. Nice bum, small waist and tan skin. When he'd first started in the business, he would have accepted her offer. Back when being desired by a multitude of women was new, not annoying.

Tina glanced at him over her shoulder and caught him watching. The light in her eye nearly made him cringe for real. Now he'd have to convince her that he might have looked, but he had no intention of touching.

The moment was interrupted when Kitty and the rest of the group burst into the room with a wave of conversation and laughter. Though he'd known they were coming, the arrival of Kitty and the entourage came with the anxious feeling he had back when he'd started out in some small off-Broadway play. Every move he made while they were around would be watched, scrutinized and reported on some social-media site if deemed interesting enough to boost his celebrity status.

He scanned the group for the winner. Kitty had texted him that she still didn't seem very excited, so he expected to find the cool smile and reserved expression from her employee photo. His scan came to an immediate halt when it landed on the smiling cutie talking to one of the cameramen.

In his mind he let out an appreciative whistle. This was not the reserved woman from the picture, not with that smile. It was what he noticed first. She had the brightest, most beautiful smile he'd ever seen on a woman. Then there were her legs: long, shapely and enticing in the short denim shorts. The lavender shirt showed off toned arms and looked good against the red undertones in her skin. Her dark, thick hair was pulled back into a ponytail.

Coming from the UK, he'd never understood the girl-next-door thing that American men went for, at least not until this moment. This woman made him think of barbecues, bike riding and picnics. All that down-home stuff Hollywood portrayed in their good ole American films.

He slowly stood and grinned. The weekend wasn't going to be as bad as he had originally thought. He'd still stick with the "look but don't touch" approach, but at least this woman was nice to look at.

She stopped talking and turned his way. The smile on her face froze, then became stiff around the edges.

She took a deep breath and just watched him for what felt like hours, but was probably just a few seconds. He waited for the excitement, frantic fanning, shriek of joy and tears. He was usually good for a tear or two.

They never came. Instead, she calmly walked over and held out her hand. "It's nice to meet you, Irvin."

That accent… Hers was a slow, husky drawl that wrapped around him and made him want to hear it whisper his name. He normally didn't care much for Southern accents, but he could listen to hers all night.

He took her hand in his. "The pleasure is all mine."

She swallowed and gave a short nod before pulling her hand back. She rubbed it across her shorts then stuck both hands in her back pockets. "I appreciate you saying that. I'm sure this is kind of an imposition on you."

"I wouldn't have offered if it were. I'm always excited to find new ways to raise money for alcohol awareness."

She nodded, but the look on her face said she didn't quite believe him. "I guess it's time for my total transformation."

At that moment, Rafael came out of his office. To see him on the street, no one would guess that Rafael was a famous photographer. His curly hair, thick square glasses and unassuming white shirt and gray khakis didn't set him apart from any other guy in his midthirties.

"Is this our winner?" Rafael asked in a loud, excited voice. He took both of Faith's hands in his and held them out. "We don't have much work to do with you. Look at those legs and that smile. You've got the cutest face, my dear."

From the way she glanced around, Irvin wondered if she was uncomfortable with the praise.

"That's very sweet coming from a man who photographs women far more glamorous than me."

"Glamour is a mirage. A mirage that I create," Rafael said, placing one of his hands on his chest. "The lens can make the meanest person look like a saint when it's in the right hands, and my dear, I've got the right hands."

Faith smiled, and Irvin was blown away by how cute she was. "The right hands and a way with words."

Rafael laughed, then snapped his fingers for Tina to come over. "If you think I'm good with words, wait until you see these pictures. Now on to hair and makeup."

"Not too much makeup," Irvin said.

Faith and Rafael looked at him with varying degrees of surprise. Though Rafael's look was tinged with a bit of curiosity. Irvin was not a makeup expert, but he had a feeling too much would only take away from her charm.

"Irvin has spoken," Rafael said. "Not too much makeup." Rafael and Tina ushered Faith to the dressing room.

"What do you think?" Kitty asked as Faith and Rafael disappeared.

"I like," he said.

"Good. She's a bit reserved. I still can't get a read on her, but I'll figure out what makes her tick."

He knew what that meant. He pointed at Kitty. "No more digging. She's here and she seems normal."

"Normal is a mirage," Kitty said, waving her hands in an imitation of Rafael that made Irvin laugh.

Several minutes later, Faith was back with her hair out of the ponytail and framing her face in a sleek bob that gently curled below her chin. They'd replaced the sleeveless lavender T-shirt with a sparkling yellow tank top and followed his instruction to not put too much makeup on her. Only enough to enhance her rounded cheeks, brown eyes and full lips.

"I'll start with pictures of you. Then we'll move on to both of you," Rafael said. He led Faith over to the gray backdrop where they'd pose for the shoot.

"What am I supposed to do?" Faith asked.

"Be your sweet Southern self, my dear," Rafael said with a wave of his hand. "Where are you from, again?"

"South Carolina. Laurel County."

"Hmm, I've been to North Carolina. Had a shoot in Charlotte once." Rafael started snapping pictures.

Faith gave him a tight smile. "That's not very close to where I'm from."

"Either way, relax, my dear. Just be yourself."

She glanced around at the background with barely concealed panic.

Irvin hurried over to her side. "Why don't we start with both of us?" He took her hand. Her palm was slick. She was more nervous than she let on.

Her eyes widened and she tried to jerk her hand away. He held on more tightly and pulled her closer to his side. "Relax."

Her hand flexed in his, and she cut her eyes toward Rafael snapping away. "Easier said than done. You weren't hustled from a plane to a photo shoot without a chance to breathe."

"Are you nervous?"

"Just a bit."

He gave her his lady-killer smile. "Don't be. I don't bite."

A frown came across her features before she lifted her chin. "That's good to know, but it's not why I'm nervous. I know I just have a few scheduled appearances with you, which is how I prefer it."

She slid her hand away and wiped it on the leg of her shorts. How she preferred it? He hadn't had a woman say she preferred spending minimal time with him since he'd left London. He started to ask why when it hit him. He'd had women try to play the reverse-psychology thing on him before. Pretend disinterest in hopes of gaining his attention. Several years ago he'd done a film in which the leading lady's character used that dishonest tactic to win over the heart of the politician he'd played. Ever since, women tried it with him constantly. Thinking she would do that was surprisingly disappointing.

"So let me guess. You entered the contest to spend a weekend with me, but are hoping to limit our time together. Not secretly hoping that something would happen between us."

Her incredulous look was almost believable. "You've got to be kidding. Do you really think I'd want to add my name to the list of forgettable women you sleep with?"

Rafael snapped faster. "Closer, my dears. You're happy about this weekend."

Irvin wrapped an arm around her shoulders and pulled her against his side. She smelled good, a light flowery fragrance. And her body fit nicely with his. A fact he wished he wasn't so acutely aware of.

"Are you accusing me," he said through his fake smile for the camera, "of planning to seduce the winner of this contest?"

She was stiff beside him, but she relaxed and pasted on her own smile when Rafael ordered her to look happy. "Honestly, the thought never crossed my mind that you'd try to seduce me. Though I doubt you'd turn down sex if I offered."

He turned to face her, almost entertained by her attempt to throw the offer out there in a backhanded way. "Oh, really. Please tell me why you think I'd take you to bed."

She hesitated, and he could tell she was wondering whether or not to say more. When determination filled her gaze he grinned. She was playing this all the way.

"You're used to women throwing themselves at you," she said. "You're linked to a different woman faster than I can change underwear, and this month *Essence* magazine's readers voted you the man women most want to sleep with. I highly doubt you turn down many offers for sex."

"Are you calling me promiscuous?"

"All I'm saying is that you don't lack for women lining up to warm your bed, and I didn't come up here to be your next electric blanket." Her voice rose on her last words. She sounded almost sincere. He struggled with wishing she was and wishing she wasn't. He no longer slept with groupies, but he had to admit, this particular one went from cute to sexy when she pretended to be angry.

It took a second for him to realize silence filled the room. They both turned to find Kitty nearly fuming, Rafael laughing and the rest of his entourage wearing expressions of disbelief.

"That's a wrap," Rafael said, balancing his camera on his shoulder.

Faith stepped away from Irvin. She looked from one end of the room to the other. "I've got to make a call. Is there a place where I can go for privacy?"

Rafael pointed to his office. "Right in that room."

"Thank you." She hurried to the office and pushed the door closed.

Kitty rushed to Irvin's side. "I told you she didn't

want to be here. I knew I should have handpicked the winner instead of using a random selection. She should be happy—"

"If you're going to say she should be happy to sleep with me this weekend, then save it. All that was a ploy. I've had women try to pull this on me before. She's probably in there right now telling her girlfriend that she's brilliant and has me fooled."

He crossed the room to Rafael's office. The door hadn't closed all the way, and he felt no remorse about eavesdropping on her conversation. He would pay money that she was in there calling someone to say the plan was working. That she was on her way to convincing him she wasn't just another fan out to land Irvin Freeman in bed.

He needed to hear it to take his mind off how incredibly sexy she'd been as she'd dressed him down. How her eyes sparked, and that accent of hers grew thicker. In that moment he imagined his name swirling out of her mouth in that drawl, and he needed to snap out of it.

He leaned close to the door, ready to hear her gloating or strategizing her next move.

"The man is exactly what I thought—another spoiled, rich playboy who thinks women are here only to please him. I told you I should have stayed home, Mama. This weekend is going to be terrible."

Her angry rant immediately proved him wrong. And for Irvin Freeman that was a first.

Chapter 5

"What are you talking about?" Virginia asked.

"I'm here and already it's a hassle. Irvin isn't the nice guy he comes across as in those interviews. He thinks I'm here to seduce him."

"Well, maybe you should."

"Mama, please don't say ridiculous things."

"Okay, that was a bit much, but it won't hurt to just let your hair down and have a little fun. You can do that without being around him."

Faith sighed and pushed the hair away from her face. Now that the shoot was over, she was pretty sure Kitty had said she was going to the hotel. She could get away from Irvin immediately.

"You're right. He'll go his way and I can walk around and explore the city a little bit before going to the party tonight."

"Can you say the word *party* without sounding like you're going to the gallows?"

Faith laughed. "Fine. I can't wait to go to the party with the arrogant actor who thinks I'm here to trick him into bed," she said with false charm and cheer.

"Goodbye, Faith," her mama said, chuckling.

"You and Daddy can call me whenever you need to. And be sure to warm up one of those meals I froze for dinner tonight. And if I forgot something on the grocery list, just call Marie and she'll get it for you. And—"

"Seriously, Faith, goodbye. Don't worry. Your daddy and I will be fine."

Faith was being overprotective, but it had been her role for the past two years. One she took so seriously she sometimes forgot they were the parents. She took a deep breath and reminded herself that her mama was a thousand times better now than she'd been when Faith had first come home, and her daddy had been living with his disability for years.

"Okay, Mama, I'll call you later."

She ended the call, then tapped the phone on her chin. Now what? She wasn't ready to face Irvin. Admittedly, she was very disappointed that he fit the entitled-guy mold. As her excitement had budded on the plane, she'd hoped he would be somewhat normal. If only Marie could have taken off work and come with her. She could relax if she had her friend along.

With a sigh, she turned and opened the door—only to jump back when she nearly walked right into Irvin. Her heart went from a tango to a standstill. The man was fine: square jaw covered by a precisely cut beard, wide, flat nose and piercing dark eyes that made her secretly swoon whenever he gave whatever lucky leading lady was starring opposite him a sexy stare.

Why, oh, why were good looks bestowed on men who didn't deserve them?

He wasn't handsome in the traditional sense. He made up for not having the classical good looks with a swagger that couldn't be ignored. It oozed from every part of him: the way he walked, talked, dressed. He was classy and dangerous, gentleman and bad boy, nice and naughty all wrapped in masculine appeal.

And he thought she wanted to get him in bed.

Well, it's not like it would be a hardship.

She gave herself a mental shake. No need thinking that. She would not be another fan tossing her panties at Irvin Freeman. No matter how seductive he looked.

"Were you listening in?"

"I was," he said in that wonderful British accent that melted women's underwear like butter on a hot skillet.

Her insides quivered. Literally quivered as if she were the virgin heroine in some medieval fairy tale. And though her virginity was long gone, something about the raw sexual energy he wore like a second skin made her believe all her previous sexual encounters were fumbling attempts at the real thing.

She crossed her arms and nailed him with the stare that used to make slacking nurses cower. "Care to tell me why?"

"I actually came over expecting to hear you gloat or come up with a new plan to flirt with me." He held up his hands when her eyes narrowed. "But I was wrong, and I apologize. How about we give it another go?" He shot her that smile. The one that tugged up the corners of his full lips just enough to tempt a woman to forget the rules and follow him to the nearest bedroom.

She held her ground and stared him down. "Why

don't we simply agree to get through the weekend with minimal contact?"

"I can't agree to that," he said.

"Why not?"

"Because I offended you, and I want to make up for it. You must understand that I meant no disrespect to you. I'm bombarded by women, as you so readily pointed out, but I don't take up every offer."

He moved closer to lean against the door frame, and his gray T-shirt stretched over made for grabbing broad shoulders. His jeans were scuffed up just enough to make them look intentionally worn. A casual outfit that seemed sexy only because the clothes were on his perfect body.

"I understand, and accept your apology. Still, you don't have to make up for it. I know this weekend is an obligation for you."

"It might have started that way, but my outlook is definitely changing."

His inviting gaze swept across her body. It was a quick and thorough examination. The kind of look a man gave when he wanted a woman to know he was interested. A look with all kinds of naughty promises. A look that tightened her nipples and sent an unexpected jolt between her legs.

"That's nice of you to say."

"I wouldn't say it if I didn't mean it. Let me make it up to you."

"It's really not necessary. Your people flew me up here. We're doing the party tonight and the premiere tomorrow. We just had an unfortunate misunderstanding, and everything will be smooth from here on out."

"Have you been to New York before?"

The abrupt change in topic threw her for a loop. "No. It's my first time."

"Then let me show you around."

Inside she squealed at the thought of getting a personal tour of the city from Irvin, but his apology and sex appeal were already making her forget that she wasn't here for a Hollywood hookup.

"I'm tired. I just want to go back to the hotel and relax. But thank you, Irvin."

He watched her for several seconds, then pushed away from the door. Before she could blink, he'd taken her hand in his. "Until tonight, then." He brushed his lips across the back of her hand.

She fought very hard not to sigh and tremble in tandem with the shivers inside her belly. "I'll see you at the party."

He let go of her hand, then motioned for her to precede him. She breathed in the traces of his cologne, clean, crisp and completely delicious, as she swept past him. When she approached, the rest of the crew tried hard to pretend they weren't paying attention, though she was confident they were doing nothing but. Kitty went into a flurry of instructions to her staff. In seconds they had their fingers flying across their phones. One even snapped a picture with his phone before typing something.

A sinking feeling went through her gut. Everything Irvin did ended up on some gossip site. Their little interaction was probably already posted somewhere. Another reason to limit her time with him. She didn't need people probing into her past and discovering what her sister had done. Her family's dirty laundry wasn't for public display.

And neither was she.

She was so ready to get to the hotel, away from the prying eyes of his staff. And from Irvin's hot glance and inviting looks.

Chapter 6

"There—all done."

The makeup artist stepped away from Faith. Kitty and several other people in the makeover squad Kitty had summoned to Faith's room swarmed closer to get a look. If it weren't for the fun of having a full makeover, Faith would have been annoyed by the way they studied her like a specimen under a microscope. But everyone on the team had been so nice and enthusiastic that she couldn't help but get drawn in.

"Perfect," Kitty said, clasping her hands in front of her. "She's a knockout. She'll look fantastic on Irvin's arm tonight."

Of course Kitty would be worried about how good of an arm piece she'd make for Irvin. But even that couldn't suppress Faith's eager smile. For the past four hours, she'd been pampered like she'd never been before. A full body massage, facial, hairstyling, makeup and even exfoliating. She blushed to think about how every single hair deemed unnecessary had been removed by the team. Through covert peeks in the mirror, she'd glimpsed some of her transformation, but now she could barely suppress her excitement to see the final results.

"Can I look in the mirror now?" She turned to do just that, but Kitty grabbed her arms.

"Not until you put on the dress."

There was a collective gasp by the team, who whispered, "The dress!"

Grinning, Faith got up from the chair and ignored the temptation to take a look at herself in the mirror. She shouldn't enjoy this so much. If she was back home, she'd think how superficial and shallow all of this really was. Right now, though, she decided to allow herself to enjoy this fantasy weekend. Besides, it was hard not to get excited over a designer dress tailored just for her. The team had taken her measurements at the start of the makeover, and the dress had arrived a few minutes ago.

She was having so much fun that she couldn't even rustle up any annoyance whenever Kitty remarked about how surprisingly easy it was to turn her into a knock-out. A comment to which she'd responded in her heaviest Southern drawl, "Good thing I got my teeth fixed a couple years back." The team laughed at her joke. Kitty only looked relieved.

Within minutes she was in the dress. They did a final gloss of her hair and makeup, and then she was in front of the mirror with an embellished "Voilà" from Kitty.

Faith's jaw dropped. The woman in the mirror wasn't Faith Logan, shift nurse and parent caretaker. The person looking back at her was the perfect arm candy for a Hollywood superstar.

The dress was long-sleeved, but there was no chance

she'd get too warm. Made of sheer material enhanced with silver stones strategically placed over her more personal areas, it clung to every curve and stopped in a wisp of material at the tops of her thighs. Full curls framed her face, and her makeup… Good gracious, her makeup was flawless. Her face shone with just the right highlights and shadows. She looked like a celebrity. In fact, she almost felt like one, surrounded by the team oohing and aahing over her appearance.

"So, what do you think?" Kitty asked with what sounded like uncertainty in her voice.

"I'm stunning," Faith whispered.

Kitty clapped and congratulated the team. "Finally, a response from you I can take."

Faith continued to stare at the stranger in the mirror… a stranger she kind of liked. If only Marie could see her now. Once again she wished her friend could have got off work to be here. She'd have to take a picture and send it to Marie and her parents. They wanted her to have fun, and this makeover was fun.

There was a knock at the door, and the excitement and buzz of conversation from the team elevated.

"That must be Irvin," Kitty said.

Faith's heart pounded like their feet on the floor of the hotel room. She broke out in a sweat. Dang it, she couldn't sweat. Not in this barely there outfit and perfect makeup. She fanned herself to cool off, but Kitty was already ushering her out of the bedroom and into the living area of the hotel suite.

Don't sweat. Don't sweat. Don't sweat, she chanted internally, as if that would stop her.

Kitty positioned her and the rest of the crew for Irvin's entrance. Vaguely she wondered if the man ever entered a room without Kitty arranging everyone on the other side of the door.

When Kitty swept the door open and he entered, Faith forgot to think, to breathe, as his sexy, dark eyes zeroed in on her. He wore a white shirt, black-and-white-striped vest and dark pants, but on him the simple clothes covered him in sex appeal. She'd heard the expression "sex on a stick" before. Standing before her, this man brought that expression to life. And she was going out clubbing with him tonight.

Don't be a fangirl. He already thinks you're only here to seduce him. Despite her warning, she couldn't help but think it would be pretty darn nice to seduce someone that good-looking.

She gave herself another mental shake. *Get it together.*

But her command fell flat when his dark gaze ran over her from head to toe, once, twice and a third time. Her body temperature soared to near nuclear levels with each sweep. He focused in on the gemstones barely covering her breasts, and her nipples immediately beaded. A slow smile spread across his full lips as he raised his gaze to hers. The look he gave her made her think about what it might be like to be his date for real. For the promise in his eye to be there not for the cameras capturing the moment, but because he was going to live up to the promise later that night.

"You look beautiful," he said, crossing the room to stand before her.

Heaven help her, she'd nearly forgotten about that voice. Desire soaked her panties. She tried to remember the annoyance she'd felt with him earlier that day. Something ridiculously hard to do with him eyeing her like that.

"Thank you," she said. She was relieved that her voice didn't waver. "I thought you'd just meet us at the club."

"A gentleman always picks up his lady at the door."

"Well, I'm not your lady. Not really. We both know this is a promotional thing." She said it to remind herself more than him.

"Promotional thing or not, I'm already enjoying myself."

He ran a hand down her arm. The flimsy material of the dress did little to block the sizzling heat of his touch. "Nice dress."

She hated herself for trembling, but it was hard to suppress. Their gazes met, and she could have sworn she saw desire in his. She blinked and glanced around at the room full of people. He was an actor, she told herself; it was his job to make women feel beautiful. This wasn't attraction and it wasn't real.

"Kitty picked it out."

"I can tell. It's not quite you."

She frowned and stepped away from his touch. Here she was thinking she was all done up to look like his perfect match for the night, and he said the dress wasn't her? True, she wouldn't have picked it out, but she looked damn good in it.

"How do you know what is or isn't me?"

"Because you don't need all of this—" his hands motioned from the top to the bottom of her dress "—to make yourself desirable. Yes, the end result is breathtaking, but your loveliness is much more subtle."

Heat flared across her skin. *Don't sweat!* Had he really called her lovely? Yes, but it didn't mean anything, she told herself, despite her fluttering heart.

"You're joking with me." She lifted her chin and stepped back.

He moved toward her, and she forgot about the crowd of people in the room watching their interaction. Awareness sizzled across her nerve endings at the subtle hint of his cologne. It was some designer fragrance she wouldn't know the name of, but it was all male. "There are a lot of things that dress makes me think about doing, but joking with you isn't one of them."

Heaven help her, he was flirting. She needed to put a stop to it before she forgot that, like the clothes and makeup, this was an illusion. He was just another high-profile guy used to getting what he wanted. From the look in his eye, he wanted her. For now. He'd quickly forget all about her come Monday morning.

She cleared her throat before she spoke. "Look, I meant what I said at the photo shoot earlier. I won a date with you through some random drawing, but I'm not here for anything more than that."

The corner of his mouth quirked up, adding a sexy tilt to his full lips. "You keep saying that, but as the winner of the prize, you could rightly demand that I do everything you request of me to make your time memorable."

"I didn't plan to request sex."

"*Didn't* implies past tense. Does that mean you've changed your mind?"

Her eyes widened. "Yes. I mean, no. I mean, I wasn't… I'm not thinking that you'd want to…that we'd…"

Heat spread across her cheeks. She held up a hand and was ready to go off on him when he chuckled.

"Relax—I'm only teasing," he said with humor in his eyes. "We're going to have a great time tonight."

Kitty hurried over. "And we're going to be late if we don't leave now."

Still thrown off by what had just happened with Irvin, Faith tried to change the subject. "What will we be late for?"

"I sent out Irvin's arrival and departure times to ensure the best photographers are there," Kitty replied.

She'd wondered earlier whether Kitty planned every move Irvin made. Now Faith had her answer. Again, the thought was disheartening. She enjoyed the new clothes, the makeover and celebrity treatment, but she could never live this life.

"Off to the limo," Kitty said. "I can update both of you on what to expect when we arrive."

"That won't be necessary," Irvin said. "It'll just be Faith and me. You and the rest of the group can follow in another car."

Everyone in the room froze. So did Faith's heart, which she was sure had decided to lodge itself in her throat. Irvin held out his arm for her to take. "I'd like to get to know my date better."

Irvin walked behind Faith to the limo and wrestled with the need to haul her against his body and explore the soft skin revealed by that flimsy material she called a dress. He couldn't keep his eyes off her thighs, the hint of a flat stomach revealed between the crystals, or the fullness of her lips tinted red and glossed against her pretty brown skin. As they slid into the back of the limo, and her dress rode up her thighs when she crossed the seat, his cock stirred in his pants. It was going to be a long night if he had to pretend he wasn't interested in doing exactly what she'd accused him of earlier in the day.

"I think Kitty is going to pop a vein," Faith said once they were settled.

He glanced back at his publicist and the pinched expression on her face before the limo door closed. "Kitty likes to be in control of everything."

"And you don't have a problem with that?"

"Her efforts, no matter how pushy, are part of the reason my career continues to be so successful."

He reached for the champagne chilling in a bucket of ice and raised an eyebrow. "Would you like a glass?"

"I guess it would be ridiculous to turn down champagne in the back of a limo with a movie star."

"Only slightly ridiculous."

She glanced at the bottle before her lips curved into a smile. "It's been so long since I've had good champagne."

"Then you'll definitely have a glass."

As he opened the bottle, she reached for her small beaded handbag and pulled out her mobile phone. He expected her to take a picture of the inside of the limo or snap a selfie with him. Instead, she made a call, then frowned.

"Problem?" he asked her.

"Yeah—my parents aren't answering their phone. It's close to midnight. There's no reason for them not to answer."

The worry in her voice pricked his concern and surprised him. Once again he'd expected her to act like any other groupie and she'd done the opposite. He couldn't remember ever going on a date with a woman who was more concerned about calling her parents than having a drink with him.

"Maybe they're asleep," he said.

"No, my parents are night owls. They watch the eleven o'clock news, then stay up for *The Tonight Show*. They should be sitting in the living room now."

"Maybe they went out. It is Friday night."

She shook her head. "No, they don't go anywhere. My mama's in a wheelchair and my dad is hurt. I take care of them and go out for them. There's no reason for them to be out."

"Is there another number to call?"

She was already dialing before he got the words out. A voice came through the other end, and her shoulders sagged with relief. "Marie, what's going on? I called home, and Mama and Daddy didn't answer."

She paused as the frown on her face deepened. "The movies? What?"

There was a bottle of sparkling cider chilling next to the champagne. He opened the champagne and poured a glass for her. Then he opened the cider and poured it into a glass for himself. He sipped his drink and watched her as she had her conversation. It was interesting that it never occurred to her that her parents might want to go to a movie. She'd said she was their caretaker. Having spent the majority of his youth looking out for his mother, he could relate. He'd worried so much about taking care of his mother and trying to save his father from himself, it had taken a tragedy for him to realize he wasn't living.

She probably deserved this weekend away more than most of the women who'd entered the contest.

Her call ended, but she continued to stare at the phone as if she were waiting for a different outcome.

"I take it you found your parents," he said as he handed her the glass filled with champagne.

She took it without really looking at him. "They went to a movie. They wanted to see the new action one with all of those stars who were popular in the '80s."

"What's wrong with that?"

"They never go to the movies." She sipped from the glass. He got the impression that she did it absently. Her mind was clearly occupied with the news of her parents' outing.

"They never go, or they never tell you they want to go?"

She spun to face him, giving him an annoyed look that only increased her sex appeal. The makeup, dress, hair were all outstanding, made her a knockout. But he'd liked her better when he'd first seen her. When she had reminded him of a life away from the limelight and argued with him at the photo shoot. The look she shot him now brought some of that woman back.

"What's that supposed to mean?"

"Obviously your parents wanted to see a movie. Which leads me to believe either your parents had an epiphany and decided it was time to break their ban on going to the movies, or maybe the more obvious choice is they decided to wait for their caretaker to leave before doing so."

She sputtered as if searching for the right words to toss back at him. "They weren't waiting for me to leave."

"So they begged for you to stay?"

Her mouth opened, then snapped shut. She took another sip of the champagne, then smiled. "My mama practically pushed me out the door. I guess I keep them from doing a lot. I just worry about them. And things have been tight." She bit her lip and looked away.

He got the impression that she regretted letting that slip out. "Tight how?"

"Not tight, really. Things have been harder because of my parents' health. I've been their caretaker."

"Is that why you're no longer the chief nursing officer in Houston?"

"How did you know that?" Before he could answer, she held up a hand. "Let me guess. Kitty."

They both laughed. "Yes. She did a check on you before calling to let you know you won."

Something flittered in her eyes before she looked away and picked at the crystals on her dress. "Not surprising. She couldn't have some crazy person winning."

"Her words, not mine."

"Did she say anything else?"

"No, I told her to stop looking into your past. You're only here for a weekend. It wouldn't be right to probe into your background like that."

She looked back at him, relief and happiness clear in her wide eyes. "Thank you for being considerate of my privacy."

He shrugged as if it weren't a big deal, but he liked it when she looked at him like that. "No problem at all."

She gave him a smile that made his heart speed up in his chest. He was definitely attracted to Faith. But it wasn't a good idea to start up anything with a woman who was around for only a weekend. Come Monday, he'd never see her again, and he shouldn't invest too much in this spark he felt. Still, he found himself asking, "So things have been tight since you moved back home to take care of them?"

She nodded and sat back on the seat. She ran a finger across the top of the champagne glass. "It's been a difficult transition. My parents were very independent, and a series of accidents have made it so that they can't be."

He slid closer to her on the seat. "Are they resentful of needing the help?"

"No, they were hesitant at first and tried to downplay the amount of help they needed, but overall they're appreciative. They think I spend too much time worrying about them and not enough time worrying about myself."

How many times had his mother pushed him to get out and live his own life instead of sticking around trying to make up for his father's shortcomings? Though he didn't regret ultimately leaving London and making a success of himself, he understood the guilt that came when you took time for yourself after giving so much to others.

"How long have you been looking after them?"

"Two years."

"Is this your first vacation since going home?"

She nodded. "It is. I still can't believe that I won. I only signed up because my friend insisted and because the proceeds benefited alcohol awareness. I saw so many patients come into the hospital who were suffering from alcohol abuse. Still, I never expected to win the contest."

"So the possibility of a date with me had nothing to do with you entering?"

She sipped her champagne and gave him a shy look from the corner of her eye. "I will admit the fantasy of it all did have some appeal."

He raised his brows and chuckled. "Some appeal. Wow."

"Oh, come on. What do you want me to say?" she asked with a laugh. "That I stayed up every night praying that I'd be chosen?"

"Not quite that, but surely you were somewhat excited."

"See, that's the problem." She pointed a finger at him, but her brown eyes flashed with humor. "You're used to women throwing themselves at you. This weekend will be good for you."

"How so?"

"You need a few days with a woman who isn't trying to get something out of you. I'm more excited about seeing the city, going to a movie premiere and trying on clothes I wouldn't be caught dead in back home than in seducing the movie star."

He placed his arm on the back of her chair, making sure to let his hand brush across her shoulders, and moved closer to her. Her eyes widened and her full lips parted with a quick breath before she looked away and finished the rest of the champagne in her glass. She might talk a big game, but Faith was attracted to him, as well.

"That's the third time you've said that. Who are you trying to convince?"

"You. I know what you're up to, sliding close to me and giving me the sexy-voice-and-eyes routine."

"You think my voice is sexy?" he asked, lowering his voice an octave.

She shook her head and laughed. "Don't go all Barry White on me."

"I'd like to go all Irvin Freeman on you," he said in his regular voice. Though he tried to keep the tone light, some of his seriousness came through.

Her smile faltered, and he saw by the warming of her eyes and the catch of her breath that she'd heard it.

"Is that what you do with your leading ladies?"

Her soft, sweet drawl slid in beneath his skin and heated his insides. It had got thicker with her question. How thick would it get if he were deep inside her?

"What I do with my leading ladies is acting. I'm not acting right now. What I'm thinking and feeling is all real."

She shifted in her seat. "I don't believe you."

"Then believe this."

He lowered his head and pressed his lips against hers, with enough firmness to let her know he was serious, but lightly enough for her to pull away if she didn't want the kiss. Her body shook, and her lips parted with a gasp. He wasn't a man to pass up an opportunity, and he took the chance to deepen the kiss.

He'd never believed in electricity or sparks igniting when a man kissed a woman, but something he'd never felt before happened as he kissed her. His skin tingled, the blood rushed through his veins, and his senses heightened to everything around them. The sweet scent of her perfume, the softness of her lips, the way she tasted of champagne—all seemed amplified. And like a man who'd got a taste of something he really liked, he dived in for more.

He put his own glass down—on the tray, he hoped— and brought his hands up to feel the softness of her hair. She made a sexy whimpering noise before her own hands came up to clutch his arms. It was on after that.

He shouldn't kiss her as if they'd been lovers for years, but damn if the woman didn't kiss well. He let his hands run across her shoulders and down her sides, which were free of the crystals and allowed the heat of her skin to sear his palms. He stopped at her hips. If he went farther, he'd find it hard to stop.

She pressed closer to him. One of her hands moved from his arm to his shoulder; the other came up to clutch the back of his head. He forgot trying to slow down then. He pressed forward, hesitantly at first, and when there was no resistance, he laid her back on the seat, his body blanketing hers. He lifted her left leg and settled between her thighs. The heat that greeted him there hardened him even more.

He trailed kisses down her neck as his hand slid up her thigh until it gripped her hip so he could pull her closer. Her body twisted beneath him; soft moans and whimpers came from her lips, each one heightening his desire.

His fingers brushed the waistband of her thong. In the back of his head he acknowledged that this was getting out of hand. That he needed to stop and get things back under control. Until her hips shifted and she moaned his name. He hooked his finger in the waistband and was ready to pull it down when her hands shoved against his chest.

"We've stopped," she said and pushed him again.

He rose, and she scrambled from beneath him to the other side of the seat. "What am I doing?" she asked beneath her breath. Her hands tried to straighten her hair and she rubbed her lips, but there was no hiding what had almost happened. She had the look of a thoroughly kissed woman.

And he wanted to pull her back in his arms and finish what they'd started.

"Faith—"

"Not now. No talking about this right now."

He reached for her, but she jerked away. The car door opened and the interior lit up with the flash of dozens of camera lights. Kitty popped her head inside. She looked from one of them to the other, raised an eyebrow and gave him a smirk that said she had a pretty good idea what had happened.

"Showtime," Kitty said. "Smile for the cameras."

He turned to Faith, who met his gaze, then immediately looked away. He took her hand and gave it a reassuring squeeze. He wanted her to look at him. He wanted more time to figure out what had just happened between them. But she pulled away and hurried out of the limo. He got out beside her and waved at the awaiting crowd, putting on his practiced smile for the paparazzi.

Chapter 7

Faith entered the club on shaky legs. If it hadn't been
for the flashing cameras outside and the constant attention of the people in the club, she was sure her weak
knees would have caused her to hit the floor. No need
to fall on her face and be the woman who'd lost all of
her pride. She was already the woman who'd quickly
become a liar when Irvin kissed her.

Smile. Walk in a straight line. Don't sweat.

She repeated her mantra to keep her mind off what
had happened. Irvin Freeman had kissed her. She'd
made out with him in the back of a limo as if they were
teenagers on prom night. And instead of being embarrassed for doing it, she kind of hated they'd been interrupted. Which was the dumbest thing she'd ever felt.
He must think she was full of crap. One minute spout-
ing off about not wanting him, then practically letting
him have sex with her two minutes later. She knew she
shouldn't have come to New York.

She lifted a hand to smooth her hair, even though Kitty had given her a quick fix before they'd entered. Between the mussed hair, wobbly legs, rumpled dress and swollen lips, it wouldn't take a rocket scientist to figure out that Irvin Freeman had already had a little fun with his prize winner.

Heat crept up her cheeks. What was she doing? Playing this game she didn't know how to handle. He'd forget all about her, and she'd return home as just the latest in the line of women who'd slept with him.

Beside her, Irvin bent over until his lips brushed the outer shell of her ear. "If you keep looking guilty, people will know that I kissed you."

She jumped and stepped away. "I don't look guilty."

"You keep checking your hair, pulling your dress and touching your lips. All the signs of a woman caught kissing."

Her hand froze in the middle of smoothing her hair. She dropped it and lifted her chin. "Point taken. How am I supposed to look?"

"Let's go for enjoying yourself."

The thing was, she wasn't sure if she could enjoy herself with all the thoughts about kissing Irvin going through her head.

"Okay, what do you want to do first?" The heated look he gave her was a sign he wasn't thinking about hitting up the bar. "I mean, who would you like to talk with first?"

"Let's get to our table. Then look around to see who else is here tonight."

The club was dazzling. Black and white tiles covering the floor, oak ceilings, leather sofas around marble tables, gold and black walls. The place was packed, and as she looked around, she had to bite her lip to stop herself from gawking at all the celebrities there. It wasn't long before they were at a table close enough to the bar to be seen but far enough away to avoid the crowd around it.

She sat next to Irvin, and the rest of his entourage surrounded the two of them. The group spoke with him but didn't really get too close.

"Are these all your friends?" she asked.

He'd leaned in to hear her question over the music. After having been covered by his body a few minutes earlier, the nearness of him sent heat skittering across her skin and wetness pooling between her legs.

"I know all of their names and the members of their families, and I spend most of my nights out with them, but no, they aren't my friends," he said. Again he spoke close to her ear, and his warm breath sent tingles through her body.

"Do you have any friends?"

His eyebrows rose, and immediately she felt bad for asking. It wasn't her business if he had friends. "Sorry, prying is one of my not-so-lovable traits." She turned away to look at the people in the club.

"I have a few friends," he said. "But for a celebrity of my stature, it looks better to travel with more than two people around you."

She spun back to him and frowned. "Are you really that conceited?"

"Kitty's words, not mine."

"You use her words a lot. Don't you ever get tired of living by your publicist's philosophy? What would Irvin prefer?"

He didn't answer. He just stared at her for several seconds. His silence made her uncomfortable. Prying and insulting him were the perfect ways to make sure he didn't kiss her again. Too bad that hadn't been part of her plan.

They were interrupted by the arrival of a group of people.

"Irvin, I thought that was you," a woman said.

They both looked up. A huge, warm grin came across Irvin's handsome face. "Selena." He stood and the two embraced.

Selena Jones was beautiful in movies but dazzling in person. Tall, thin, with the grace of a ballerina, the Brazilian actress was most men's fantasy. And the woman reportedly linked to Irvin.

"This is Faith Logan, the lucky winner of a weekend in New York with me," Irvin said after he and Selena broke apart.

"It's nice to meet you, Faith," Selena said, a genuine smile on her perfect face. "May we join you?"

"Of course." Faith slid over in the booth. What was she supposed to say? *I just kissed your boyfriend, so it might be kind of awkward*?

Irvin slid in next to Faith, with Selena on his other side. Faith prepared herself for an evening of watching the two lovebirds completely ignore her. Instead, Selena drew her into conversation, and the rest of the group at their table brought up the next film Irvin and Selena were going to start shooting in Canada the following week. Selena didn't seem possessive of Irvin or unfriendly toward Faith, and before long, Faith forgot about feeling awkward and began to enjoy herself.

The entire experience was like a dream. Rappers, models, actors, singers and reality stars all came by the table to speak. Some she loved, others she hated, but after having a conversation with a hip-hop mogul and his superstar wife, she was thoroughly starstruck.

She could even forget for a few minutes that she'd easily fallen under Irvin's spell in the limo when her favorite television star asked her if she wanted to dance.

After shaking her body on the dance floor, she was introduced to an R & B singer she'd idolized since her teenage years. She knew she'd be embarrassed later for nearly crying when she met her and going on about how she'd related to her albums since her first one came out when Faith was fourteen. But thankfully, the singer accepted Faith's fangirl moment with aplomb and even laughed when Faith joked about trying to dye her hair platinum blond to be like her.

She stopped short of asking if she could take a picture with the woman, but was grateful when someone else suggested it.

After snapping the picture, Faith didn't care how much of a Kool-Aid smile she had on her face as she walked to the bar and ordered a bottled water.

"You're so lucky," a woman said next to her.

Faith turned to the woman, who was tall and curvy with long, dark hair highlighted blond. Faith recognized her as one of the women who'd been hovering around Irvin's table in hopes of taking a picture with him.

The woman grinned, revealing even white teeth. "You won the weekend with Irvin. I entered one hundred times and didn't win."

Faith's jaw dropped. "A hundred times?"

"Yeah, but I'm a big fan." The woman lowered her eyes and flicked her long hair over her shoulder. "Anyway, I just wanted to say congratulations. Enjoy your weekend."

"Yeah, thanks," Faith said. The woman gave her a tight smile, then walked away. Faith shook her head. *One hundred times?* She'd known Irvin had a big fan base, but to enter the contest that much... Faith couldn't imagine living with so many people obsessed with her life.

Irvin strolled over with two guys. She recognized one as the singer Dante Wilson and the other as a professional basketball player. She didn't follow basketball and didn't know his name, but he was hot right now and in every commercial out there. Dante was dressed casually in jeans and a screen-printed T-shirt, while the basketball player wore dark pants, a white shirt and a gray blazer.

Irvin gave her a smile that nearly melted her like hot candle wax. It seemed like the kind of smile a guy wore when he spotted his woman. Happy, bright, promising that even better things were sure to come. He was such a good actor, because it couldn't be genuine, but his smile made her wonder what the weekend would be like if it were.

"You haven't asked for a picture with me, yet you seem to float in the air when you take a picture with every other celebrity," he said with mock hurt.

"What can I say? Tonight's been amazing."

He turned to the guys. "Faith, I'd like you to meet Dante Wilson and Jacobe Jenkins. Gentlemen, let me introduce you to Faith Logan. She is the beautiful woman you both were asking about earlier, and she also had the misfortune to have her name selected as my date for the weekend."

The guys chuckled before directing their attention to her. Their appreciative looks threw her off. She couldn't believe she had three handsome, rich and single men all focused on her. Nor could she believe the two newcomers had asked about her. And if they had, what on earth had Irvin said about her?

"Very nice to meet you, Faith," Dante said. "You're the lucky winner. You must be very excited that your name was selected."

"It was a surprise," she said. "I only entered to support the foundation. I really didn't expect to win."

"But it isn't too much of a hardship," Jacobe said with a grin.

"I wouldn't be so sure," Irvin cut in. "On the way over, she was telling me her only reason for entering was to support the cause. I'm fairly sure she would be just as excited if I were completely cut from this entire weekend."

"Oh, really?" Dante asked. "Not many women say that. Maybe you're just what he needs."

"That's doubtful," she said. "I'll leave on Sunday, and this will just be another packed promotional weekend for him."

Jacobe smirked. "You've already made a big impression on my man. I think he'll remember this weekend."

The comment froze her insides. She quickly got an idea of what Irvin might have said to them about her. They must know about the kiss and how quickly she'd contradicted herself. She gripped her bag, embarrassment and anger coursing through her body. Why she should have expected him to keep what had happened to himself, she didn't know. There was nothing special between them. She was just another groupie for him to have a little fun with. Of course he would tell his friends what had happened.

"Are you having a good time?" Dante asked.

"Actually, I think I need some air. A few minutes away from all this would be nice. Is there anywhere to go that isn't as crowded?"

"You can go on the roof. There's seating up there, but

only a few of us have access, so it's not as crowded," Irvin said. "I can take you."

She didn't want to go somewhere less crowded with him, but she had little choice. "That'll work. Then you can come back down to the party. I'd like to be alone."

He frowned, and his friends exchanged looks. "Excuse us," Irvin said. He took her elbow and led her away from them. She immediately pulled out of his grip. She felt his gaze on her, but she didn't meet it. She'd made a mistake falling for his charm earlier. She was not going to do it again.

Faith followed Irvin to the office of the club owner. He was a tall, handsome man with golden-brown skin and the smoothness that came with spending his time catering to the rich and famous.

"I'd like to go to the roof, Calvin," Irvin said. "My date needs some air."

Calvin raised a brow and gave Faith a brief once-over. "Well, this is a first. Follow me."

The statement seemed odd, but she didn't have time to consider it. She just wanted to get out of the heat and the crowd and then dismiss Irvin back to Selena and his friends. Maybe they'd all have a good laugh about the country girl who easily fell for his lines.

Calvin took them through a door in his office that led to a staircase. He smiled at Faith, a kind and genuine smile, and she couldn't help but return it. "Enjoy the view."

Irvin placed a hand on her back and directed her to the stairs. She tried not to focus on how good his hand felt through the skimpy material of her dress by reminding herself that he'd bragged about kissing her to his friends.

She failed miserably.

They walked out onto the roof, and Faith gasped. "It's beautiful," she said. White lights were strung around the roof, and small lanterns cast a soft glow on the cushioned chairs. The music from the club played softly in the background, allowing the few people there to have intimate conversations. The shining lights of the New York skyline added to the view.

"I'm surprised everyone isn't up here," she said, following Irvin to one of the vacant cushioned seating areas, but they didn't sit.

"Calvin only grants a few people access. It's where I come when I need a break from the crowd and whatnot."

"Why only a select few?"

"Because it's for those who really want to escape the attention. Not for people who just want to say they have access to another exclusive area of a club."

She glanced around at the skyline. The breeze blew her hair in her face, and she tucked it behind her ear. "You must not use it often." When she glanced back at him, he wore a confused look. "The 'this is a first' comment from Calvin."

"He didn't mean me. He meant I brought you. It's rare to bring someone who doesn't have access with you. Too easy for a person to brag about being part of the so-called 'in crowd.'"

"How do you know I won't brag?"

"For some reason, I trust you won't. It doesn't seem your style."

The softly spoken words, the night air and the twinkling lights were all sucking her back into his spell. She turned away before she found herself in his arms again.

"You can go back to the club now," she told him. "I'd rather be alone."

"I'd rather stay and find out why you're suddenly acting so cold." He made a motion to a server she hadn't noticed standing off in the shadows. When the guy came over, Irvin ordered a bottle of champagne.

"I'm not being cold," she said after the server walked away. "And if I were, it's not like you don't deserve it."

"Because I kissed you?" He sat down.

She crossed her arms. "That and because it's obvious that you let the rest of your celebrity group know about it. Did you have a good laugh about it, or did you make bets on how soon you'd score?"

The server returned with the champagne. He uncorked it and poured two glasses before melting back into the shadows. All the while, Irvin clenched his jaw, and she could have sworn there was frustration in his eyes.

"I didn't tell them about what happened in the back of the limo," he finally said, reaching for his glass and sipping while looking away from her to the beautiful view.

"Really? Then what was the comment about you not forgetting this weekend?"

"I told them both to back off when they asked about the sexy woman on the dance floor." He looked at her and said it as casually as he'd ordered the champagne. "I didn't like that, and I made it known."

"I'm not yours," she said. Her breathless voice gave away the whirlwind inside her that his words had stirred up.

"Maybe not." He took a sip of the champagne but watched her the entire time, his dark eyes seductive in the low light. "But after that kiss, I find myself wishing you were."

The breeze might as well have come from a hair dryer;

it did nothing to cool her off. Her heart pounded like the bass of the music. Unable to trust her knees, she slowly sat on the edge of the seat and reached for her own glass.

"You're teasing me again," she said. "And I don't like it." It was one of the biggest lies she'd ever told. She liked what he'd said way too much.

"I'm not teasing you. I believe in fate, destiny, whatever you want to call it. It's the reason you're here this weekend instead of some mindless groupie."

"I don't believe in fate. If it's real, fate is good at kneeing you in the stomach and laughing at your pain. The only thing that brought us together was a random drawing."

"A random drawing doesn't explain this attraction… or that kiss."

Why, oh, why did that man have to say *kiss* like that? Silky smooth and soft enough to make her immediately remember how good his lips had felt on hers.

She didn't answer, couldn't answer. She couldn't explain the attraction. Sure, he was a sexy-as-hell movie star, and most women in America would have taken PMS for life for one night with him. But she'd never been drawn to a man just by his looks. If she'd come here and Irvin had turned out to be the jerk she'd first taken him for, he might as well have been Freddy Krueger. But he hadn't. He'd been nice, kind of funny and able to laugh at his own celebrity. He'd apologized for his assumption and had been nothing but charming and honest since then.

But she couldn't fall for it. She'd thought she'd found a total package before, and he'd turned out to be runner-up for asshole of the year. So what if there was a spark of attraction? Come Monday, Irvin would be off to Canada with his on-again, off-again, beautiful costar.

"Unless…" His words broke into her thoughts. "…you kissed me because of who I am. Unless it isn't attraction on your end, and you are just another woman waiting to go home and tell everyone you almost made love with Irvin Freeman in the back of a limo."

"That isn't why I kissed you," she said quickly. "I wouldn't do that."

"Then why?" He slid closer. The man knew how to penetrate a woman's defenses. She couldn't keep her guard up when he was so close to her. "Did you kiss Irvin the star, or did you kiss me because you feel this thing as much as I do?"

Her insides quivered. Desire blossomed between her legs, and she held her champagne flute with shaky hands.

"I feel it." When he moved closer, she slid away. She faced him and shook her head. "But I don't trust it. This isn't meant to be more than a weekend of fun. I don't want to be that girl you slept with on a promotional weekend, and I really don't want to walk into something that might hurt me in the long run. I don't know your true dating history—just what's printed in the tabloids— but I can guarantee a weekend fling wouldn't change your life as much as it would mine. I can't handle that."

His dark eyes searched hers. Then his gaze moved away to follow every feature of her face. He finally smiled and brushed the back of his hand across her cheek. "I understand. So, we'll have fun and get to know each other over the weekend."

"Without the kissing."

"I'll try, but I make no promises." The smile he gave her made her want to sigh and melt into his chest.

He leaned back in the chair. "Tell me about your life before your mum got sick. Do you miss it?"

"Sometimes. I loved my job in Houston. It was challenging and was taking me on the fast track to success. But honestly, it wasn't until I came home and started working as a shift nurse that I realized how much I missed working with patients."

"I take it from your surprise about the movies that you don't go out much. Did you before?"

"In Houston I did. Fund-raisers, galas, luncheons. Every weekend there was some reason to get dressed up and hit the town." She glanced down at the crystals on her dress sparkling in the low light. "Though you were right about one thing. I wouldn't have gone out in this dress."

"Was there a guy? Is there a guy?"

"There was a guy." She frowned. "We split after I came home."

"The distance?"

"No, the sleeping with the woman who took my old position. She fit his image more."

"Was he a celebrity?"

"No, worse—a man with political ambitions," she said with an eye roll. "He was the county treasurer, and as chief nursing officer, I had a lot of connections with our legislative delegation. He dated, then married the state senator's daughter who took the job after me. Now Corey is state treasurer."

She swallowed her champagne to push back the bitterness she felt. She hadn't missed Corey as much as she'd expected when she returned home. A part of her accepted that their relationship was coming to an end. She just hadn't expected him to jump in bed with another woman the same week she said she wasn't coming back.

"Then he's a prat."

"A what?"

"Idiot."

She nodded. "Well, prat or not, he's history," she said. "Now it's a quiet life for me."

He nodded, a serious expression covering his handsome face. "Must be nice. I'm always running from one place to the next, always in front of a camera. Sometimes I miss the anonymity I had before I was famous."

"That's a lie and you know it."

His eyebrows drew together. Maybe she'd overstepped her bounds by saying it, but that prying part of her was popping out again.

"Why would you say that?" he asked.

"I watch enough television to know some celebrities get more media attention than others. And the ones who get the most cater to the cameras and paparazzi. Kitty and your entourage prove you're a caterer."

"It keeps my career relevant."

"It keeps you in the public eye."

"That doesn't mean I couldn't be happy with a simple life. Maybe on a farm with a wife, kids and a dog?"

She actually laughed out loud. "Now you're confusing yourself with the guy you played in that movie last year. I can't see you as the farmer type at all."

He didn't seem to take offense at her laughter, and he actually chuckled. "You're right about the farm. But I do get tired of the constant pressure. I'm trying to break into directing. Start my life behind the camera instead of in front of it."

"Would you be happy with that?"

"Yes," he said without hesitation. "I needed to reinvent myself, and I have. Now I want to get back a bit of the Irvin I was before. I wouldn't be a farmer, but I could see myself in some secluded house in the country. No longer having to make club appearances and being known for how many shirtless scenes I have in a movie."

"You had to predict the fame that would result from being an actor," she said.

"The thing is, I didn't expect to become such a success. I came over to America and needed a job, any job. A mate suggested I make easy money being an extra in this play. I liked it, so I tried for a few parts and got them, surprisingly. Then I met Kitty, and before I knew it, my career took off."

"You can always walk away from it for a while and pursue directing."

"It's not that easy. I'm supposed to be in Canada next week to start filming another movie."

"Then walk away after that."

His eyes narrowed in on her before he turned away and put down his champagne glass. He'd taken a few sips but didn't drink it all. She hadn't said anything, but she noticed that he'd drunk cider in the back of the limo. She wanted to ask why but decided not to. Getting to know him too personally wasn't part of the agenda.

"Let's get out of here," he said.

She thought of going back into the crowded club. Sure, she'd had fun mingling with the stars, but right now she enjoyed the quiet. And her conversation with Irvin.

"I guess we should get back to Kitty," she said.

"No, I mean let's get out of here altogether. Just the two of us."

Faith hesitated. She didn't trust how comfortable things felt between them. Being alone with him made it easy to forget that. "I'm not sure."

"Would you rather leave with Kitty?"

She cringed and shook her head. "No."

"Then trust me."

He held out his hand. She met his gaze as her mind seemed to jump back and forth from her preconceptions about him to the man he really was. "Is that possible, to leave without her?"

"I don't just dream of walking away from the spotlight. I've found ways to avoid it."

"How?"

"New York is a massive city. Anyone can become a face in the crowd."

She was in New York with a handsome movie star who wanted to show her a good time. Hadn't she promised herself she'd enjoy this weekend? Pushing aside her worries, she put her hand in his.

The smile he gave her was dazzling in its intensity. "Come on, cutie. I'm going to show you how I walk away from it all."

Chapter 8

"We'd like to leave," Irvin said to Calvin.

The club owner stopped scrolling through his tablet and looked up at them from the seat behind his desk. He didn't speak for a few seconds, just looked between Irvin and Faith. Though his expression was blank, Irvin knew Calvin thought he was out of his mind. If he were Calvin, he'd think the same thing. The private exit out of the club was kept private for a reason. Letting Faith see it not only compromised other celebrities' ability to leave by avoiding the waiting crowds but also compromised Calvin's reputation of being able to offer that service to his most distinguished clients.

Irvin hoped his instincts were right about Faith. He believed she wouldn't run to the media and talk about everything that happened this weekend for a few extra dollars.

Calvin finally set the tablet on the desk and rose from his seat. "I'll show you out."

Faith gave Irvin a questioning look that he answered with a smile. Calvin led them to the other door in his office, which opened to an empty hallway. At the end of the hallway was a freight elevator.

"You know your way," Calvin said to Irvin. He turned to Faith. "I'm sure we'll meet again."

Faith gave him a doubtful look but held out her hand. "It was nice meeting you."

"Tell Kitty I'll call," Irvin said to Calvin.

"I'm afraid one day she's going to really hurt me for doing this." But Calvin's grin said he wasn't afraid at all.

The two men shook hands, and as Calvin went back into his office, Irvin placed his hand on the small of Faith's back and guided her down the hall to the elevator.

"Where do we go from here?" Faith asked.

"We take the lift down to the basement, which is connected to the building behind the club. From there, we go up another lift into that building and exit."

"Won't Selena miss you?"

Irvin laughed. Selena was probably busy doing her own exit. "No, she won't miss me."

Faith looked down the hall toward Calvin's office door and back at the elevator, a frown on her cute face. "And no one knows celebrities sneak out this way?"

Irvin pressed the button to open the elevator door. Once inside, he inputted the code for the basement and turned to her with a grin. "So far we've been good. Paparazzi stalk the entrance and marked exit on the side of the club, but they don't tend to walk around the block to see who's coming out of this building."

The ride down was swift. They exited into the brightly lit basement and crossed through another door into the connecting building. From there they got on another lift and took it up to the first floor of the adjacent building.

"How do you keep people from seeing you leave from here?"

"Calvin owns this building. It has offices and event space he rents out on the top floor. If there was an event going on, he would've warned us. Otherwise, it's normally empty on the weekends."

He pulled off his jacket and passed it to her. "Still, you'd better put this on. No one will be able to ignore you in that dress."

She slid her arms into the sleeves, which went well past her wrists, and pulled it tight. Immediately he missed the enticing sight of her skin beneath the sheer material. Thankfully her sexy legs were still visible.

"No one will know who I am regardless of this dress. But how in the world can you stop people from noticing you? You're the most wanted man in America."

He stepped close to her. Close enough to smell her sweet perfume and see that her eyes were a lighter shade of brown than he'd originally thought. She tugged the jacket closer around her. She looked both nervous and expectant. He'd promised not to kiss her again, and he would keep that promise. For now.

He took a pair of shades out of the pocket of his jacket. When he stepped back, she quickly looked away. He wasn't sure if it was relief or disappointment she tried to hide. He then slid out the hat he'd tucked into the back of his pants and pulled it low over his eyes.

"Am I inconspicuous now?" he asked, holding out his arms.

She covered her mouth and laughed. "Hardly. I don't see how anyone wouldn't recognize you."

He took her hand and led her down the hall to the

front of the building. "Because no one is looking for me. Just wait and see."

"I take it you slip in and out of places unnoticed quite often."

"It drives Kitty crazy."

As expected, the adjacent lobby was empty except for one of Calvin's security guards at the front desk. He gave a slight wave to Irvin before pressing the button to unlock the front door. It was well after two in the morning, but so close to Times Square there were still plenty of people on the sidewalks. The honks of horns from the vehicles in the crowded streets punctuated the night.

He wrapped an arm around her shoulders and pulled her close to his side. They joined the crowd on the sidewalk. He expected her to pull away. Instead, she wrapped an arm around his waist and fell into step with him.

"I'm surprised you didn't tell Calvin he wouldn't be seeing you again."

She kept her head down as they walked. "I figured saying that would only increase his discomfort. It was pretty obvious he wasn't tickled by the idea of letting me use your secret exit. He must really trust your judgment."

"He was one of the first people I met when I moved to New York. He knows I wouldn't put him out like that if I wasn't sure what I was doing."

"I was thinking," she said. "He could charge whatever he wants for secret exits and secluded rooftop tables."

"Calvin opened his club as a place for adults to hang out without a bunch of young kids starting a fight every night. He didn't expect it to become the celebrity hangout it's turned into." His own regret crept into his voice. Calvin's club had risen in popularity at the same time Irvin's fame had.

"He can't dislike that completely. It's made him successful."

"True, but he's a private man who has cameramen hanging around his business constantly. He understands the need for an escape."

"I guess I can understand that."

She lifted her head and looked around, an eager smile on her lips. "Are we going to Times Square?"

Her excitement was infectious, but first he had to make sure no one had spotted them.

"Eventually. I haven't yet worked my magic to blend into the crowd."

She chuckled. "What's next? A fake mustache to go with the shades and hat?"

"Something more subtle," he said. Then he slowed. "We're here."

"This building?"

"No, this corner."

Irvin walked over to a man sitting on a bucket at the side of the building. He had a patched-together easel in front of him and used charcoal to sketch the surrounding buildings and street corner.

"How's it going, Carl?" Irvin said to the man.

Carl stopped sketching and grinned, revealing a crooked-toothed smile. His brown suit sported a few worn spots, and in the dark Irvin couldn't tell if it was clean.

"My man Freeman. I was wondering if you were coming by tonight," Carl said, leaning his elbow onto his knee.

"You almost didn't get me," he said, taking one of the buckets next to Carl and flipping it upside down. "I had to go to a party."

Carl took a look at Faith beside him. "Skipping out on me for a hot date?"

"You could say that." He pulled Faith forward. "Faith Logan, this is Carl."

Faith smiled and reached out her hand. "Nice to meet you, Carl."

Carl grinned first at Faith then at Irvin. "She's pretty, and Southern, too. Where are you from, Faith?"

"South Carolina, the Upstate near Greenville."

Carl nodded and crinkled his brow. "I've been to Charlotte before."

Faith chuckled. "That's North Carolina, but that's okay."

"There's nothing like a Southern girl, Freeman. You better treat her good tonight."

Faith gave Irvin a quick glance. "He's done well so far."

Irvin's brows rose. "A compliment! I should have taken you away from that party hours ago."

"I don't mind giving them when they're deserved. Not just because they're expected," she said with a cute grin.

Carl leaned forward. "This is the first time Freeman has introduced me to one of his lady friends. It's a special occasion."

Faith gave Irvin another one of her shy glances. "Is it, now?"

"Mind if we sit with you for a while?" Irvin asked.

"Not at all, Freeman. I'll even draw your picture while you're here." Carl was already pulling down the canvas with the landscape and putting up a blank one that was propped against the building behind him.

Irvin looked from Carl to Faith. "Do you mind?"

Her mouth twisted into a half smile, and she shrugged. "Why not?"

Right then and there he realized he was right to trust her. Many women wouldn't enjoy sitting on a corner with his nearly homeless friend. She hadn't hesitated or batted an eye. He was liking her more and more each minute.

"Looks like you've got a client, Carl," Irvin said.

Carl rubbed his hands together. "Then have a seat and let me get started."

Irvin sat on the overturned bucket.

"Where's the lady gonna sit?" Carl asked with a grin.

Irvin took Faith's hand and pulled her down into his lap. "It can seat two."

Faith wiggled on his lap. "You think you're sly."

"I'm too direct to be sly. I just like the idea of you sitting on my lap."

Carl chucked. "My man Freeman."

"Did you go by the place today, Carl?" Irvin asked.

Carl shook his head and began sketching. "Not today."

"You know it's there waiting whenever you're ready," he said.

"I know, Freeman. One day I'll take you up on it."

"One day soon, I hope," Irvin said.

Faith gave him a questioning look, but he shook his head. With a nod she turned back to Carl. "How long have you been drawing, Carl?"

That was all it took to get his friend started. Before long, she had him telling stories about all of the interesting things he saw while sitting on corners around the city, drawing pictures. The more she conversed with Carl, the more Irvin believed fate had selected her to win his contest for a reason.

Whenever he left Calvin's club, he'd sit beside Carl and blend into the background. His friend normally camped out here on Friday nights, especially if he knew Irvin was going to be in the vicinity. People didn't pay much attention to two guys sitting on a corner drawing sketches of the city. He'd watched several cameramen walk right by, too busy looking for Irvin in the crowd to notice him right beneath their noses.

It was a welcome moment of quiet, but tonight Irvin couldn't enjoy it as all of Faith's soft curves in his lap drove him mad. Every time she shifted, his erection swelled. It brought back memories of how her body had cushioned his earlier in the limo and made him want to do a lot more than have her sit on his lap.

Faith shifted again, bringing her bum firmly against his erection. She froze, then tried to move away. He gripped her waist and pulled her back. He watched her pulse flutter at the base of her neck. She brought a hand to her chest and rubbed as if she were having a heart attack. He could relate. His heart pounded hard, too.

She kept talking while he watched her. The people passing by, the hum of the city—all became nothing. There was only Faith, her soft body and her sweet fragrance.

Suddenly she jumped from his lap. "Sorry, Carl, I'm getting a back cramp," she said, rubbing her lower back.

"I got a good start," Carl said. "I can finish this later and give it to Irvin the next time I see him. I think you're clear to take off, Freeman."

Reluctantly Irvin stood. "I did promise to show her Times Square," he said.

"You've never seen Times Square before?" Carl asked.

Faith shook her head and stuffed her hands into the

pockets of his jacket. "I have not. I've traveled throughout the Southeast, but this is my first trip to New York."

"Then he better show you a good time," Carl said.

Irvin wrapped his arm around her shoulders. She didn't stiffen or pull away, just relaxed into the embrace. He didn't think too hard about how much he liked it. "I'll make sure she does."

He pulled out his wallet and took out several bills. "For the portrait."

Carl shook his head. "You know you don't have to pay me."

"Still, I want you to have it." He held the money out, but when Carl hesitated, Irvin dropped the bills in Carl's art case. "I'll see you around, Carl."

"You two have a good time," Carl said with a wave.

Faith waved back as he led her away. "Have a good night, Carl."

"You too, beautiful," Carl called back.

As they walked in silence Irvin tried to make sense of what he was feeling. He'd experienced lust before. But this was different. He didn't just want the woman beside him. He wanted to get behind the walls she surrounded herself with. Even though she'd kissed him back, she'd wished she hadn't. She didn't deny that there was an attraction between them, but then she asked him to ignore it.

He was a man and a celebrity; he'd had his share of weekend flings. She was right—he easily moved on afterward. He never had an urge to keep up with the woman once the affair had run its course. Faith was wrong about one thing, though. He doubted he'd walk away from an affair with her without consequences. Faith wouldn't be so easy to dismiss from his thoughts.

"Do you always give him money?" Faith asked after several minutes.

"Not all the time. Sometimes I bring him food. It's nothing."

"Your nothing probably is a big something for him." They walked in silence for a few more minutes. "How did you end up hanging out with him?"

He shrugged. "It just kind of happened. One day I was trying to dodge a cameraman and saw Carl sitting there, drawing. I tossed my coat in the trash, slid on the hat I keep in my pocket, sat down next to him and asked for a portrait. He studied me for a while, then told me I needed to face him more so he could get a good angle. That put my back to the cameraman, who walked right by us." They paused to let traffic through, then crossed 34th Street. "Another day I left the club early but saw a few paparazzi on the corner. They don't know about the exit, so they didn't notice me. I walked a few blocks, and there was Carl again. Then I started noticing him around the city. If I could, I'd sit with him, and if I couldn't without attracting attention, I didn't. We started talking after a while, and here we are."

"Does he realize who you are?"

"I don't think he did at first. Then one day he said I resembled a guy in a picture he found and pulled out an issue of the *New York Post* with a picture of me."

"What did you say?"

"Just said it was interesting."

"And he hasn't ratted you out."

"No, he hasn't."

"Where's he from?"

"New Jersey. He lost his job, family and home because he's an alcoholic."

"Has he stopped drinking?"

"He struggles with it. It's why he's still homeless. I rented a place for him, but he only goes there when he's sober." Irvin took a deep breath and pulled her closer. "He hasn't been in weeks. I'm hoping one day he'll stay for good. But he's got to do it on his own, you know. I learned that watching my father."

"Your dad drinks?"

He shook his head, trying to shake out the regret of his past. "My father drank. He died ten years ago."

"I'm sorry. Is that why you try to help Carl, because you couldn't help your dad?"

He stopped and turned to stare at her. They were almost in the heart of Times Square, but he didn't notice the lights or the noise. Just her beautiful face and her softly seductive words punching right to the heart of something he never wanted to admit even to himself.

"Maybe, in a way. I know from experience you can't make someone struggling with addiction quit unless they want to."

"No, you can't." Her voice rang with regret. Then she shrugged. "But it's nice that you're trying to help him."

"What can I say? He lets me hide out with him, so it's the least I can do."

The smile she gave him was brighter than all the lights surrounding them. "I think you're all right, Irvin Freeman." She leaned up and kissed his cheek.

He ran his hands up her arms, wishing he could feel her skin instead of the jacket. "I think we better get moving before I show you how to really break that no-kissing promise we made earlier."

She didn't reply, yet her eyes said she wanted him, too. He lowered his head. Anticipation at tasting her lips again urged him on. A group of people bumped into her as they passed. She jerked forward, and he placed a steadying hand on her arm as the rest of the group of twentysomething kids rushed by. They wore T-shirts with Greek fraternity letters and chanted what must be their mantra. Faith rolled her eyes and grinned.

"Oh, to be young," she said.

He returned her smile, while inside he hated that the moment was broken. "Come on. Let's see the bright lights of the big city."

Chapter 9

It was after four when they finally left Times Square. Faith had to admit it was a sight to behold at least once in a lifetime. And once was about all she needed. Even this late, the Square was as bright as daylight and so crowded it hummed with an excitement that she felt in her bones. They'd managed to blend in with the crowd. Every time people gave him a double take and looked ready to ask if he was who they thought he was, he and Faith were able to blend into the crowd first.

They'd sat and watched the people, he'd bought her an outrageously good cupcake from a local bakery, she'd flirted with a police officer at the NYPD station beneath lit billboards higher than any building back home, and they'd even given tips to the street performance artists. Though why you had to pay to take a picture with someone who invited you to take one, she still didn't quite understand.

"You know that's a racket," Faith said. They were walking down Broadway, back toward her hotel. The crowd and excitement from earlier were fading away as the night turned into morning.

"What is?" He had his arm around her shoulders. During the walk, she'd snaked her arm around his waist.

She didn't know when it had happened, but somewhere between the rooftop and her cupcake, she'd lost her apprehension about opening herself to him. His sense of humor, the way he didn't make a big deal out of his celebrity, his kindness. Her plans to not get close chipped away like cheap nail polish.

"The people in Halloween costumes or body paint asking for tips to take their pictures," she said.

"I don't belittle anyone's hustle," he said.

"I get that, but the one guy who just painted his face silver and could barely walk wanted me to give him five dollars for a dance. No, sir."

Irvin's smooth laugh filtered through the early-morning air. "I'll agree with you on that. But that lady did deserve a tip."

She slapped his stomach with the palm of her hand. "You would say that." She thought about the woman who was naked except for pink-and-blue body paint, a G-string and a showgirl headdress. Faith couldn't imagine doing that, but had to admit it took guts to put it all out there for the whole world to see. "Maybe she did deserve something," she agreed with a laugh.

"Did you enjoy yourself?"

"I did. Seeing Times Square on television doesn't do it justice."

"So you'll be back?"

She shook her head. "Not for a while. It was fun, but way too crowded for me."

"You can come to New York and not go to Times Square."

Making a return trip was the problem. It would take a lot of time and funds she couldn't spare to plan a vacation for her and her parents here. "Who knows when I'll make it back to New York?"

He stopped and turned her to face him. "Maybe you'll have a reason to come back quickly."

Was he hinting that *he* would be that reason? The idea touched her heart and set off an intense pang of longing. They'd had a wonderful night. Admittedly, there was a spark between them. Maybe if they were in the same social circle, or it was remotely feasible that a movie star would fall for a small-town nurse, they could actually become a couple.

Standing there with her hands in his and still wearing her designer dress, she could almost pretend that this could work.

"Maybe I will."

His eyebrow quirked, desire flared in his eyes, and the corner of his lips rose in the smile that melted female hearts from New York to New Delhi.

He lowered his head, brushed the tip of her nose with his, and her breath caught. She wanted him to kiss her. Screw it—she wanted him to do a lot more than kiss her. The way she was feeling, she wondered if she should take this fantasy as far as it could go.

Dark eyes stared into hers. He tilted his head and leaned in close. His lips barely brushed hers when a loud clang startled them both. They jumped apart and turned to the noise. Faith's heart pounded, not from the noise but from the broken anticipation of kissing Irvin again.

A couple who looked to be in their late fifties were bent over trying to pick up hundreds of tiny sheets of paper. A metal bowl, which must have held the papers, spun in fast circles before it finally stopped.

The few people still on the street with them hurried past without helping. Faith frowned and rushed over.

"Can I help you?"

The couple exchanged a look before eyeing her warily, but that didn't stop Faith from bending down and picking up the various scraps of paper.

"Thank you so much," the woman finally said. She had kindly blue eyes, and her salt-and-pepper hair was pulled away from her face by a headband. She wore a long-sleeve white shirt and slim-fitting blue jeans.

"It's no problem at all. If I were at home, everyone who saw this would have stopped to help."

"Where are you from?" the man asked. He was trying to get the pieces that had fallen into a puddle in the gutter.

"South Carolina."

"Ah, I should have known," the woman said, smiling. "The accent. I have a cousin who lives in Atlanta. Have you been there?"

Faith laughed and shook her head. Apparently South Carolina didn't exist to people in New York. "Yes, but it's about three hours from where I stay."

By then Irvin had come over and got the last pieces of paper and the metal bowl. They placed the handful of dirty papers into the bowl then handed it to the lady.

"Now they're ruined," the woman said with a sigh.

"It'll be okay. We'll rework them as we go," the guy said, though the tone of his voice didn't support his reassuring words.

"What were they?" Irvin asked.

The woman pointed to a shop next to them. "This is our flower shop. And these—" she held up the bowl

"—were the greeting cards for our orders today. Our girl who normally writes them quit suddenly, and we spent the night putting them together." She looked at the guy and sighed. "All of that work."

"Can't you rewrite them as they go out?" Faith asked. She had no clue about how a flower shop operated, but she assumed it shouldn't be too hard to scribble a few lines before attaching them to a bouquet.

The guy straightened his shoulders. "Of course not. We are Belles Fleurs. We create beautiful bouquets, and they're accompanied by a card with handwritten calligraphy. We can't just write them quickly."

"I've ordered flowers from you before," Irvin said. "Your cards are your signature."

The man grinned, apparently mollified by Irvin's recognition. "Then you know the effort that goes into each bouquet."

"I do. And I know your cards. Calligraphy, when done correctly, is beautiful. I learned it myself several years ago."

Faith turned to him with wide eyes. "Seriously?"

"Yes."

Faith put a hand on her chest. "I used to practice calligraphy until it was perfect. When I was a teenager I used to dream about sending a handwritten love letter like a heroine in one of those Victorian novels. Or receiving one from some dashing hero." She shrugged and chuckled. "Now I use the art to write out my yearly Christmas cards."

A moment passed between them. Another area of common ground and similarity. She saw in his eyes that he was falling deeper into this, too. Or at least, she hoped that was what she saw. She'd hate to be in this on her own.

"Then you realize we have a lot of work to do before we open," the woman said. "Thank you again for helping us."

"Wait a second," Faith said as the woman began to turn away. "We can help."

"I beg your pardon?" Irvin said.

"Excuse me?" the woman said simultaneously.

"We both know how to write in calligraphy, and you need to rewrite all of those cards. We can help."

The woman and man exchanged another look and eyed them from head to toe.

"It's obviously been a late night for you two," the woman said. "We appreciate the offer but—"

"I'm not tired," Faith blurted out. "Irvin, are you tired?"

His eyes lit up and he grinned. "Not at all."

They both turned to the couple with a smile. The woman slowly returned it before shrugging and glancing at the guy. "Xavier, what do you think?"

"I need to see their writing first, but any help would keep our orders on time today," he said with a wave of the hand.

Faith clasped her hands together. "Then let's get to it."

"These are excellent!" Xavier exclaimed two hours and two espressos later.

Faith shook out her hands and smiled. "It was kind of fun to write all the different notes."

"There are a lot of people in love out there," Irvin said. He too stretched out his fingers.

Xavier grinned. "That is one of the reasons I enjoy owning this shop. Every day I get to help a couple express their love for each other." He looked at Irvin. "And to thank you for your help, your next bouquet for your girlfriend is on me."

Irvin gave Faith a smile that would melt ovaries. She jumped down from her stool in the front of the flower shop. The next girl he bought flowers for wouldn't be her.

"I couldn't take them for free," Irvin said. "Not after learning exactly how much work you all put into these bouquets."

Faith pulled out her cell phone and checked the time. "Wow, it's past six thirty." She looked at Irvin. "Kitty's supposed to be at my hotel room at seven."

They'd stayed out all night. She couldn't remember the last time she'd stayed up all night and it wasn't work related. College, maybe. But she'd never had this much fun, and it had everything to do with him.

"The itinerary can wait," Irvin said, standing. "You need to get some rest."

"What about you?"

"I'm used to being on set for long hours. This was nothing."

He muffled a yawn as he said it, and they both laughed. Now that the excitement of helping out Xavier and his wife, Diane, was waning, she was starting to feel the fatigue set in. The caffeine in the espressos had nothing on a body not used to staying up partying.

Diane came from out back, where the truck had just arrived with the latest batch of flowers for the day. "All done?" she asked. "You've got to let us buy you both dinner or do something else to say thank you."

"Yes," Xavier quickly agreed. "We would still be working right now without your help. And look at how beautiful you both write. I may ask you both to come back again."

Something close to disappointment flashed across Irvin's face. The same emotion blossomed in Faith's chest.

"Tonight was a onetime deal for me," she said with a forced smile. "I go back to South Carolina tomorrow. But if I'm ever back in New York, I'll definitely come by again." She walked over to Diane and held out her arms. "I'm from the South, and we do hugs."

Diane grinned and hugged her. Then Xavier did the same.

Irvin shook Xavier's hand. "I'll ask around about people with calligraphy skills to help you fill that position."

Faith never would have expected him to agree to assist in the first place, but offering to help them find a replacement was even more than he needed to do. Heaven help her, in less than twenty-four hours he was making her fall for him.

"That's too much," Diane said. "You have to let us give you something. Xavier, do something."

Irvin walked over and placed his hand on the small of Faith's back. It sent a rush of pleasure across her skin. She could get used to him touching her. "What's your favorite flower?"

"Nothing fancy or exotic. Roses are my favorite."

He turned to Xavier. "You wouldn't have a dozen for my date, would you?"

Faith waved her hands. "That's not necessary."

Xavier patted her arm. "Never stop a man from giving you flowers." He hurried across the room to a refrigerator filled with flowers and came back with a beautiful bouquet of red roses. "This isn't enough to pay you back for what you've done."

"It seems like adequate payment to me." Irvin raised a brow at Faith. "For you."

"Perfect." She couldn't say any more.

They made their way to the front of the store, but Diane stopped them at the door. "Before you go I just… wanted to ask. I mean…you look just like him. Are you…Irvin Freeman? The movie star?"

Irvin gave his showstopping smile. "Guilty as charged."

Diane squealed and squeezed her husband's arm. That started another round of thank-yous and questions about what they could do to repay him and Faith. All of which Irvin gracefully declined.

"You are full of surprises," Faith said as they walked the last few blocks to her hotel. The sun was up, and the streets were slowly filling again with early risers. "I got carried away when I offered to help them. You could have said no."

"I thought it was sweet that you were so quick to jump in. Do you always do that?"

She thought about the way she volunteered for the assignments no one else wanted and how back in Houston she was the one to dive in and organize the fundraisers at the hospital. Then how she easily gave up her life there to come home and help out her parents.

"Yeah, I guess I do."

"And who helps you, Faith?"

She shrugged. "I don't need any help."

"Everyone needs help now and then."

"I manage," she said. A glance at his face told her he was about to argue. The truth was, there'd been several times she'd wished she'd had help. Wished that her sister hadn't stolen money from their parents or that there was someone who could help her care for them.

She loved them dearly, but some nights it just seemed so overwhelming.

"We're here," she said as they approached the hotel.

They stopped at the door, where Irvin took her free hand and pulled her around to face him.

He grazed the finger of his other hand across her cheek and down her neck. The featherlight touch sent out a warning that she was nearing dangerous territory. He was going to kiss her. And she wanted him to.

"I had a good time tonight," she said.

He pulled her closer. "So did I."

"I appreciate your effort to make things fun. I know this probably wasn't your ideal Friday night."

"It's going to be hard for future Friday nights to live up to this. I've discovered that my date has a big, caring heart." His eyes lowered to her lips. When they flicked back to her eyes, they simmered with desire. "And even though we keep getting interrupted, and I promised not to, I'm going to kiss you."

"Maybe I should go inside and make it easy for you to keep your promise."

He rubbed the sensitive skin of her wrist. The other hand brushed the side of her neck. Her brain turned to scrambled eggs.

"Walk away and I'm likely to follow you and drag you into my arms."

It felt like slow motion as he slid his arm around her waist. His fingers pressed into the soft skin of her back while his erection pushed against her stomach. Desire infused her bloodstream, heating her body, while her breaths became shallow, as if she were coming down with something. Not surprising. The need in his eyes was contagious.

"I must be dreaming," she whispered.

"No, cutie, this is no dream." And then his wonderful lips gently kissed hers.

She sighed softly, then tentatively ran her tongue across his full lower lip. He groaned but didn't push forward. He tasted like the peppermint gum he'd chewed in the flower shop. His tall body was as solid as the city skyscrapers and as hot as the streets in summer. He completely enveloped her in his strong arms. Everything about the kiss—his firm lips, the brush of his beard on her face, the hard press of his body and slow glide of his tongue—was divine.

Her hand gripped the front of his shirt and tugged him forward. The roses were crushed by their embrace, their sweet fragrance surrounding them. Oh yeah, she was definitely getting into this. The tension in his body snapped, and he kissed her back with an urgency that made her core tremble. Long fingers sank into her hair, which had become frizzy sometime during the long night. His hands tightened, and he turned her head to deepen the kiss. The pull of his hands in her hair, combined with the pleasure of his mouth on hers, sent her body on a dizzying ride. Proof that something wonderful could get infinitely better.

Would he make love as well as he kissed? She could find out. She could actually succumb to this need and know what it was like to make love to him.

"Oh, no, not out here on the stoop. Anyone can snap a picture and splash it all over the internet before we get upstairs." Kitty's voice broke them apart. "And where have you been? For God's sake, we've got to be ready to leave in less than two hours."

They jerked apart. She tried to breathe as Kitty approached, talking nonstop about the stupidity of disappearing from the club and reappearing kissing in front of Faith's hotel. Embarrassed, and reminded that she was only here as a publicity stunt, Faith stepped away from Irvin. She couldn't look at him. Couldn't forget this wasn't real. It was time to get back to reality.

Chapter 10

Faith's blaring cell phone jarred her from sleep. It was at the highest volume, the setting she'd put it on last night in the club in order to hear it if her parents called. Now she wanted to slam the phone with a hammer and never get another call again.

After poking her head out from the mound of covers and groping around the nightstand, she finally grabbed her phone and answered it.

"Why do you sound as if you're asleep?" her mama asked.

"Because I was asleep." Faith rubbed her eyes and pushed herself up against the headboard. Kitty had thankfully agreed to cancel the morning plans so that Faith could be rested for the premiere that night.

"It's ten o'clock. You never sleep this late. You must have been up really late last night. Partying until the break of dawn with a handsome movie star."

"I wasn't partying until the break of dawn," Faith said through a yawn.

"Maybe you ended the night seeing the sights…or kissing in front of a fancy hotel."

Faith was suddenly wide-awake. She sat forward. "What are you talking about? How would you…?"

"Know that you spent all night roaming New York City with a movie star and ended it kissing in front of your hotel? Marie called me because a picture of the two of you was posted on the internet this morning."

"We thought we were away from the cameras," Faith said. Had they been followed the entire night?

"Honey, when it comes to celebrities, you're never away from the cameras. According to the article, someone at the hotel snapped the picture with a cell phone and sent it to the website. I doubt half the story is true."

"What does it say?"

"You two were spotted at the club, left early and turned up at your hotel first thing this morning. I must admit, I wouldn't have believed it if I hadn't seen the picture myself. Are you two a thing?"

"No, Mama, we're not a thing. I leave tomorrow, and he's going to Canada to shoot a film next week. We just got caught up in a moment."

"Men like that don't get caught up. They know what they're about." Virginia's voice brimmed with warning. "Now, I'm not telling you to not have any fun. I want you to enjoy yourself. Snatching a kiss or two from Irvin Freeman isn't a bad thing. Just remember that when all the glitz and glamour is over, you're coming back to real life. Don't get too caught up in all the fantasy."

Faith ran a hand across her face before sighing. "I know that. Believe me, I do."

A few seconds passed before her mom spoke again.

"You've had a hard time moving home from Houston and giving up everything."

"And I'd do it all again. I love you and Daddy. I wouldn't just sit by and let you two struggle after what Love did."

"But you haven't done a lot for yourself. You haven't dated anyone since you've been home."

"I haven't had time to date," she said.

"You need to start dating again. It'll be good for you to go out with some nice guys around here. Start having fun."

And not fall for an actor who'd be shooting love scenes with Selena Jones the second she left, Faith added silently.

"Sounds like you and Daddy are having fun," she said.

"We just figured since you were off having a good time, we'd take advantage and do the same."

"Take advantage? Mama, seriously, if you wanted to go to the movies, I would have taken you. You don't have to wait for me to leave town."

"Well, you're always so worried about the bills, then saving whatever's left to make up for what Love took. *You* don't even go to the movies."

"Okay, I get it. But that doesn't mean I want you and Daddy to feel like we can't enjoy ourselves. We'll start going to the movies, and we can even eat out every once in a while."

"And you'll go on a few dates, too?" Her mother's voice was hopeful, almost desperate.

Now guilt crept in to join the embarrassment she felt from earlier. Thanks to the internet, her mama was now worried about her. "Yes, I will find a nice guy to start dating."

They chatted for a few more minutes before getting off the phone. Faith still had several hours before Kitty was coming back to get her ready for the premiere. Irvin had convinced Kitty to abandon the plans for a tour of the city today so they could both get some rest. Apparently it would be a long night of partying after the premiere.

In a way, she hoped it was. Maybe being surrounded by people instead of spending time alone with Irvin would help her do exactly what her mama suggested. What she knew she needed to do. Not get wrapped up in the fantasy, and not believe that the attraction between them could turn into anything more.

She put her phone back on the nightstand and lay back on the bed. Her phone rang again just as she pulled the covers over her head.

She frowned at the unfamiliar number, though she recognized the New York area code. She'd bet anything it was Kitty. No doubt the woman couldn't really let everything on her itinerary go.

"Hello?" She didn't bother to hide her frustration.

But the voice that answered her was not Kitty's. "Get out of the bed, come downstairs and meet me."

Irvin's tone sent a quiver through her body. She jumped up in bed and looked around the room as if he'd magically appear.

"I thought we were resting," she said.

"That's what I told Kitty to get her off our backs. I'm going to give you a tour of the city and deliver you to her capable hands in time to prep you for the premiere."

"Why would you do that? Kitty already had it planned out."

"Kitty and the rest of the entourage I don't want. This way it'll be just you and me. Now hurry up. We've got about thirty minutes before someone who recognizes me reports back to her and she comes after us."

She flipped the covers back and hopped out of the bed. "I can't get cute in thirty minutes."

"You're cute already, and much cuter without all the makeup they put on you last night. Just throw on some shorts, because I love your legs, and get down here." His voice was filled with a contagious enthusiasm.

She laughed and hurried to the closet. "I'll be down in no time."

"It must be nice to order up a ferry for two people."

Faith turned from the side of the ferry, where she watched the Statue of Liberty, to look at Irvin standing beside her at the rail. The wind whipped her hair around her face, and she continued to try to smooth down the strands. Irvin turned to her, too, and gave her a grin that was both overconfident and sexy.

"We could have waited in line for tickets," he said.

"Oh, no, I'm not complaining. I just wouldn't even know where to start to get my own ferry."

"Call it one of the perks of celebrity. Besides, I wanted to show you as much of New York as I could before tonight."

"Are you nervous? About the premiere?"

He shook his head. "A little," he said, leaning his forearms against the railing. "But at this point there's little I can do about it. People will either love the movie or hate it."

"Does it bother you if they hate it?"

"It used to. Not anymore."

She sensed a story behind the reason. "What changed?"

He shrugged as if it were no big deal, but he didn't turn her way. "My mother was always proud of what

I'd become and how quickly I found success. When I lost her, I lost the only person whose opinion I really cared about."

Faith nodded, not knowing what to say. She'd never been any good at speaking the right words when someone talked about a deceased parent. She remembered how all the well wishes people had sent her way when her mama was sick provided only a small amount of comfort. Useless words didn't do much to ease the pain.

"When you put it like that, I guess I can understand," she said. "When my mama got sick, my dad had already been out of work for two years because of a back injury. Then my sister—" She stopped, not prepared to reveal that private shame. "My parents had some financial trouble," she said instead. His eyebrows rose at that information, but she pressed on. "So I came home to fix things. I don't know what you know about nursing, but I went from the top of the food chain to almost the bottom."

"Why'd you have to do that? With your background, you should've been a shoo-in for the top position in your small town."

She laughed as she reached out once again and tamed her hair. She really wished she'd gone for the ponytail today. "I'll let you in on a little secret about small county hospitals. When certain nurses get a top position, the only thing that gets them out of it is death. Despite my qualifications, there wasn't anything available for me. Everyone expected me to be bitter about the change in circumstance. And for a month or two, I was." She glanced at him and raised a brow. "Pay cuts aren't fun."

"What changed your mind?"

"My mama. It was soon after her stroke and she still couldn't do much for herself. I'd worked the night shift and come in to give her a bath. She took my hand and squeezed." Tears burned her eyes at the memory. She turned her face to the wind to dry them. "She said thank you. The look in her eye said it was for more than just the bath. Right then and there I knew that if I had to do it again, I would."

"You mentioned a sister. Where is she?" he asked in a solemn voice.

Faith gripped the rail. "In rehab."

"Who's paying for that?"

"I am," she said in a clipped tone.

She glanced at him out of the corner of her eye. He looked ready to speak, but instead turned away to look at the view, a frown on his face. Maybe he was weighing his options just like her. Wondering how much to get involved.

"We're almost there," he said. He pointed, and she followed the gesture to the dock. "Are you sure you don't mind skipping a visit to Ellis Island?"

She nodded. "I don't have a name to look for. I just want to see Lady Liberty."

Though he'd sneaked away from Kitty, his bodyguard still accompanied him. She was glad for that, because it wasn't long after they got off the ferry at Liberty Island that people began to recognize him. Though the crowd didn't swarm him, there were more than enough people who came up for pictures and autographs. Irvin was nice to everyone, smiled for the cameras and signed the scraps of paper they produced before quietly asking to be excused to enjoy the view.

Despite the constant interruptions, she enjoyed being there. They managed to take their own pictures with the Manhattan skyline in the background, and they continued to laugh and talk as they walked around the monument. She loved the way his hands moved when he talked. He was so expressive when he got onto a subject dear to him. This wasn't acting, and she loved seeing him that way.

"You're so good with your fans," she said once they were back on the ferry for their return trip.

"They're the reason I can give you a private ride to the Statue of Liberty," he said.

He reached over and took her hand, threading their fingers together. Her shortness of breath had nothing to do with the wind whipping around them. Slowly he pulled her to him, the warmth of his body and the seductive scent of his cologne invading her senses. She expected a kiss; instead, he pulled her back against his chest and wrapped an arm around her waist. They stood that way for the rest of the ride.

When they docked, he took her uptown to Central Park. The only thing she wanted to see was the Bethesda Fountain.

"It's in all the movies. I've got to see it," she said.

"Then we'll see it," he said with a laugh.

They sat at the fountain, eating hot dogs and sipping sodas. Every once in a while his bodyguard had to push back fans, but for the most part Irvin accepted their requests with a humble smile. Throughout it all, he told her about his fascination with New York.

"It always seemed like this fantastic place," he said, spreading his arms to take in the city. "Full of energy and life. I needed that. I'd had so much energy drained out of me before I left home."

The need to understand why was like a physical tug in her stomach. She didn't know much about his past. She was a fan, but she didn't belong to any fan club or read everything she could about his life. She knew that he'd grown up in London, that his life there had been rough before coming to America and getting a break-out role ten years ago.

Knowing more about him and his past would only pull her in more. But staying detached was growing harder with each second she spent with him. His humor, his attention and even the way he insisted his bodyguard keep her away from the attention of his fans all endeared him to her. So instead of asking why, she changed the subject.

"What's next on the tour?"

He glanced at his watch. "We don't have a lot of time, but I wanted to take you to the Top of the Rock. I've arranged for us to get private access, so that should speed up the process."

She looked at a group of women who were obviously debating coming over to ask if he was really Irvin Freeman. "If you're tired of being out and about, we can go back."

He only smiled and shrugged. "It comes with the territory. Besides, I don't often get the chance to give a beautiful woman a tour of the city, even if it's a modified tour."

With the constant New York traffic, it took a while for his driver to get them to Rockefeller Center, but thankfully the celebrity perks of private elevators got them through the rush and to the top in no time. She was blown away by the magnificent views, rendered speechless.

"We were there," she said, pointing to the Statue of Liberty in the distance. They went to the other side of the building, and she pointed to Central Park. "And there."

He'd not only got them a private elevator but also

somehow worked it out that tourist trips to the top were stopped while they were there. It was the first time all day they weren't accosted by starstruck fans, and she noticed the difference in him. The lines around his eyes disappeared, and his laugh came a little easier. Being recognized might come with the territory, but she doubted Irvin enjoyed the constant attention.

When they got on the elevator to leave she pulled out her cell phone to record the blue-and-purple lights in the clear elevator ceiling, which made her feel as if the elevator was going warp speed up and down the shaft.

"What are you doing?" Irvin asked.

"My mama would love to see this," she said, holding the phone above her head.

"Then bring her back and let her see it. I'd be happy to arrange another private ride."

His voice held an invitation that went further than just helping her mama go to the top of Rockefeller Center. Her heart beat faster than the speeding elevator.

"I'd have to see," she said. "You're so busy, you might not have time to set something up."

"I'd make time for you."

His dark eyes held hers captive. The promise she saw there made her mouth go dry. Could he really mean it? Would he really make time for her after this weekend was over?

The elevator stopped and the doors opened. As they prepared to get off, a guy moved to get on. She recognized him as Lincoln Harris, the anchor of the news show she watched every week with her parents.

Faith grabbed Irvin's shirt with one hand and pointed at Lincoln. "Oh my God, it's you!"

Lincoln's eyebrows rose, and he smiled behind his signature dark-framed glasses. "It's me."

"I love you! My mama is gonna flip when I tell her I saw you. We watch you every weekend." She turned to Irvin and grinned. "Can you believe it? It's Lincoln Harris." She spun back.

Lincoln looked at Irvin and held out a hand. "Good to see you, Irvin. Good luck with the premiere tonight."

"Thanks, Lincoln." He placed a hand on Faith's back. "This is Faith Logan. She's my date for the weekend."

"Lucky you," Lincoln told Irvin with a wink. He wasn't in one of the signature suits he wore behind the news desk. Instead, he wore a plain white T-shirt and dark jeans. The gray hair at his temples only added to his sophistication.

"It was nice meeting you, Faith," he said, holding out his hand.

"Same here, Lincoln." She took his hand and pumped it up and down, giving him a big grin as he got on the elevator and they exited.

"You're excited to meet every other celebrity but me," Irvin said with a laugh. "I'm starting to get offended."

"Oh, please. I was excited to meet you. But I watch Lincoln every week. He's part of our routine."

Irvin took her hand and pulled her into the crook of his arm. "I see that now I'm going to have to become a news anchor so I can enter your living room every week."

The gesture was so familiar, so comfortable, that she didn't hesitate to slip her arm around his waist as they started walking toward the exit.

"I guarantee the news ratings would go through the roof if you did that."

"Who cares about ratings?" he said. He leaned over to her ear. "I only care about making you scream my name the way you just did his."

A tremble raced through her body. "You don't need to be on the news to do that."

His sexy grin turned her insides to lava. "What do I need to do to make you scream my name?"

Kiss her. Run his hands over every inch of her body. Make love to her as if she were the most beautiful woman on the planet. That was all it would take. She'd scream his name, and probably lose her heart at the same time.

But she couldn't tell him that. Instead, she said, "Wouldn't you like to know?" Then she hurried toward the exit before she succumbed to the temptation in his eyes.

Chapter 11

The lights of cameras temporarily blinded Irvin as he exited the limo at the Ziegfeld Theater in Manhattan for the premiere. He smiled and gave a wave before turning back to the limo and reaching his hand out to Faith. When she smiled at him, something hitched in his chest. Again, Kitty and the team had done a fantastic job prepping her for the premiere. There would be only a handful of men who would be able to keep their eyes off her tonight in the black-and-silver dress that dipped low between her breasts and stopped midthigh.

Faith's warm brown eyes met his, and her lips curved up into a soft smile. He gave her hand a squeeze and wished he could climb right back into that limo with her and go someplace private. Movie premieres were necessary in his line of work, and usually he enjoyed them. But right now, he'd take another escape like the one they'd shared last night. Just him and Faith.

He couldn't remember the last time he'd had such an easy relationship with a woman.

"Are you ready?" he asked.

She got out of the car and froze when the cameras flashed in her face like minibursts of lightning, casting them both in blinding bright lights.

"Wow, this is crazy." Her voice was filled with awe. "Do you ever get used to this?"

"Not really." He pulled her close and wrapped his arm around her waist.

Her body stiffened, and she tried to pull away. "They'll think something is going on between us," she said past a stiff smile.

"Isn't there?" he replied, raising a brow.

"But… I mean…we aren't really together."

"Tonight, you're mine."

Her lips parted. Only the flashing lights kept him from kissing her the way he wanted to. It had been less than twelve hours since he'd kissed her in front of her hotel, but it felt like years.

"Okay," she said, though the look in her eyes was unsure.

Before he could reply, Kitty was already rushing them forward. They went through the motions of smiling for the cameras and interviewers, stopping every few feet on the red carpet. Faith tried to step back—Kitty even tried to help her get out of the way—but Irvin wouldn't let her. He meant what he said. She was his date tonight, and he didn't want her hidden in the background.

During the interviews, he introduced her as the lucky woman who'd won the weekend with him.

"So you're really going to hate going home tomorrow, aren't you?" the ultrathin female correspondent for an entertainment show asked Faith.

"It will be difficult after such a great weekend," she said with a good-natured smile.

"What about you, Irvin?" the correspondent asked. "You'll be on your way to Canada for filming next week. Are you excited about the project?"

He wasn't excited about it. It was another action role that would require him to be shirtless, holding a gun and kissing Selena. He'd made the decision to send his screenplay to the producer the second he signed the contract to play the part. Once again, anxiety trickled down his spine. He still hadn't heard from Kevin.

But he kept all those thoughts to himself and told the reporter what she and his fans wanted to hear.

"I'm very excited. I've worked with Selena Jones before, and she's brilliant."

"You two really turn up the heat whenever you're on set," the correspondent said.

He rubbed his chin to remind himself not to roll his eyes. "All I do is stand there. She brings enough heat on her own," he said. It was vague enough to play up their upcoming movie without confirming anything. It was how the Hollywood machine worked. You had to keep up the buzz for the movie. It was how you sold tickets.

"I bet she does," the reporter said with a wink to her cameraman.

When he heard members of the cast being called together for a photo, he stepped back. "If you'll excuse us…"

He pulled Faith close and walked toward the rest of the cast on the red carpet. Faith didn't relax into his side the way she had earlier. This time her shoulders were stiff, and the smile he'd come to enjoy was replaced by a slight frown.

"You all right?"

She glanced at him out of the corner of her eye and nodded. "I'm fine. Just not used to the cameras and interviews."

He could understand. After ten years, it was still overwhelming to him, though in Faith's case he had a feeling it was more than that. "I didn't think about that."

"If you don't mind, I think I'll stay out of any upcoming photos. People are here to see you, not me."

He stopped and turned to face her, taking her hand in his. "But I'm very glad that you're here."

Her smile returned, though it didn't quite light up her eyes. "Thank you."

Kitty and the photographers called his name. He gave her hand a squeeze, then leaned over to kiss her. She turned her head at the last second so that his lips brushed her cheek. She didn't look at him when he raised his head.

He took pictures with the rest of the cast. The romantic comedy was filled with the top African-American actors of the day, and during filming it had been more like a large family gathering on set instead of a job. So the smiles in the pictures and the laughter during the interviews were all real and easy. But he couldn't keep his eyes from straying to Faith, who now hung in the background with Kitty watching.

Dante arrived, accompanied by screams from the women in the crowd and another flurry of camera flashes. Irvin was in the middle of an interview with another entertainment show with his on-screen girlfriend when his friend strolled over to Faith. Within a few seconds he coaxed a laugh and smile out of Faith. Irvin frowned as he watched the two. He wasn't the jealous type. After all, in Hollywood there was no need to be jealous, because if your date found another guy interesting, there were always more women waiting in the wings. But now he felt an odd feeling rev up inside him as he watched Dante and Faith smile for a picture together on the red carpet. A voice inside him yelled "Back off."

"If you'll excuse me," Irvin said, ending the interview in the middle of a sentence.

He ignored the startled expressions of his costar and the interviewer to cross the short distance to Faith and Dante.

Kitty stopped him midstride. "What are you doing?"

"I'm going to get Faith away from Dante," he said and tried to brush past.

Kitty grabbed his arm. He spun to tell her to let go, but she held up a hand. "Be careful there. She isn't what she seems."

"What are you talking about?"

"Her family is swimming in debt, and I believe her sister is the reason. I know you like her, but be careful."

"I know about her financial issues."

Kitty let him go. "You're always a target, Irvin. Don't let her Southern charm and sweet smile fool you."

Irvin restlessly tugged on his jacket and he processed her words. Faith wouldn't open up about her financial issues, but did that mean she was trying to deceive him?

He nodded at Kitty, who seemed to relax when he acknowledged her warning. Slowly he crossed the red carpet to Faith and Dante.

"Dante, how's it going?" He looked from his friend to his arm around Faith's shoulders and back.

Dante's eyebrows rose, but he also quickly removed his arm from Faith's shoulders. "It's a great turnout, Irvin. This movie is going to be a hit." He didn't have to say anything, but from the understanding in Dante's eyes, Irvin knew he got the message. *Keep your hands to yourself.*

"That's what the critics say." He glanced at Faith. "Are you ready to go inside?"

She nodded. "Is it time already?"

"Yes. We've done all the interviews and got enough pictures."

"But the real fun," Dante said, "will be the after-party I'm throwing at the Standard hotel."

She grinned at Dante. "You're throwing the after-party?"

"I throw the best parties." Dante looked at Irvin. "I'll see you both after the show."

"Are you having fun?" Irvin asked Faith.

"I am." He could see that her excitement from earlier was back. He hated that Kitty's words now made him question the reason. "Your life is so busy. A premiere today, then off to shoot another film in a few more days. When do you leave?"

"Monday."

"The day after I go home." The brightness of her smile dimmed. "Tomorrow will go by so quickly. I should tell you now that I had a great time."

"So did I."

Their eyes met. The end of their weekend together was coming soon. Could he really be feeling this connection to her, or would it go away once they separated? Was it all a ruse on her part, or was she genuinely the woman he was falling for? The one who helped people, hadn't asked him for anything and hesitated whenever they seemed to get close? He'd spent years studying people, learning their expressions to imitate them. He watched her and didn't see deception. Kitty might have told the truth about Faith's family, but he didn't believe

Faith planned to ask him to do anything about her financial situation.

Why did he have to let her go? Why couldn't they stay in touch? Why couldn't he date her? He knew plenty of celebrities who dated people from outside the industry. But she'd have to put up with the spotlight. Would she want to for him? The question unbalanced him. He'd never had to worry about a woman choosing not to be with him, and right now he was really worried that she would.

They went into the theater and were seated up front with the rest of the cast. As the movie played, he could tell it was a hit. He normally spent time watching his performance and critiquing what he could have done better. This time he found himself watching Faith's reactions. Celebrating when she laughed, and feeling completely satisfied when she gasped appreciatively at his shirtless shower scene. The same happened with the love scenes. As he watched her, his body heated quickly to its flash point. He imagined kissing Faith, holding her naked against him, filling her, bringing her to climax. He saw her chest rise and fall rapidly with her short breaths as she stared at the love scene playing out on-screen. Her tongue continued to dart out over her bottom lip. Then she twisted in her seat and looked his way. Her eyes widened when they caught hold of his.

He didn't care about the theater being crowded. Or about the stories already floating around of him kissing her outside of her hotel, or being unsure if she was willing to see where this would go. He had to kiss her.

He leaned over and brushed her lips with his. He felt her body tremble as her soft sigh caressed his face. Her eyes closed, and her lids sparkled in the dark lights of the theater. The gentle kiss wasn't enough. He'd just gone in for a real kiss when Kitty cleared her throat beside him and kicked his foot.

He glared at his publicist, who only gave him an innocent look. He got the message. There was no need to cause a stir at the premiere. But he didn't like it. He turned back to Faith and whispered, "Later."

He watched the battle in her eyes before she looked back at the screen. She was still afraid to trust what was happening between them. He trusted it. Before the night was over, he planned to make sure it would last longer than a weekend.

The movie was great, and the after-party was definitely jumping. The hottest DJ mixing all the hits, a view of the bay and skyline that was out of this world, A-list celebrities everywhere, even a hot tub that had her wondering where people got bathing suits from. Yet Faith couldn't have a good time. She gave a good show of enjoying herself, smiling, taking pictures to show her parents and trying not to wince whenever someone brought up how hard it would be for her to go home at the end of the weekend.

Irvin wasn't making it any easier. He kept her by his side, almost as if they were a couple. He'd already thrown her off by saying tonight she was his. But could she really be his for one night and move on? She'd have to. So the bigger question was, did she really want to be his for the night?

Umm, yeah!

The thought sent her heart into a frenzy.

She lifted up onto her toes so she could speak into Irvin's ear over the music. "I'm going to get a drink."

He turned away from the group they were talking with, which included Dante and Jacobe Jenkins.

"I can get it for you," he told her.

There he went again. Treating her like a girlfriend and making it harder for her to resist sleeping with him before this weekend ended.

"No, thanks. I just need a second."

Concern flashed in his eyes, and she had to turn away quickly. *Tonight, you're mine.* His velvety voice ran through her head.

He stopped her from walking away by taking her hand in his. Slowly he brought it up and lightly brushed his lips across the backs of her knuckles. Desire darkened his eyes.

"Don't go too far," he said in a voice laced with heat.

Breathe. Now was the time to breathe. Her lips parted with a shaky breath as she gently pulled her hand away. She didn't need to look over her shoulder to know he watched her walk away.

She strolled out onto the open area of the rooftop club. The New York skyline framed the well-stocked bar. The woman who'd congratulated Faith at the club the night before stood at the end of the bar. She smiled and waved. Faith lifted a hand and wondered if the woman found her way into every party Irvin attended.

"I see the way he's looking at you." Kitty's voice came from behind her.

Forgetting the superfan, Faith asked the bartender for water. No need to further cloud her judgment with alcohol.

She faced Kitty. "I don't know what you're talking about."

"Still playing coy," Kitty said with a smile. "There's no need. Irvin is smitten with you, and I haven't seen him that way in all the years I've known him."

"He's not smitten." She slowly turned her head to peek over her shoulder. Irvin watched her and Kitty.

"He's definitely something for you."

The bartender handed her a bottle of water. She quickly twisted the cap off and took a gulp of the cool liquid.

"He can have any woman he wants," Faith said after she wet her mouth.

Kitty nodded. The lights from the party made the red streak in her hair appear to glow, and she looked fantastic in a sexy black dress. "He can, but he wants you. Normally, I try to keep away the groupies and gold diggers. I may whore him out to the media, but I don't believe in setting up women in his hotel room. But you're different."

"Are you saying you want to whore him out to me?" Faith said in a tight voice.

Kitty held up a hand and shook her head. "No. What I'm saying is that normally he picks the women he wants to sleep with covertly, but he's been very open with laying claim to you."

"He isn't laying claim."

"He stopped midinterview with *Entertainment Tonight* because you were talking to his friend, a known ladies' man. He's kept you by his side all night, sneaked away from me and the rest of the team twice to be alone with you and kissed your hand before you walked away. Face it. He's laying claim."

That reminder to breathe would have been useful now. Air struggled to find its way into her lungs. "I leave tomorrow."

"We'll see. Either way, if you're going to become the girlfriend of Irvin Freeman, I'll work on promoting you, as well. We'll play the good-daughter angle, move you and your family to New York and set you up in style."

"Whoa, wait a minute. I'm not moving to New York. And just because there's some kind of spark between me and Irvin doesn't mean I want to become caught up in this publicity parade. I like my privacy."

"Like it or not, you're about to lose it. You're going to be the most envied woman in America, and everyone is going to want to know what it was about you that won his heart."

If people dug into her past, they'd learn about her twin and the money she'd stolen from her family. Or worse, Love might skip out on rehab and try to take advantage of Faith's relationship with Irvin.

"I'm just a weekend fling. Come Monday, I'll be another woman who was linked to him briefly in a long list of women."

"Maybe, but I doubt it." Kitty's eyes narrowed, and she leaned in. "So if there is anything you're hiding that may hurt his career, you need to spill it. From where I'm standing, you're his newest fling, and I need to know everything and have a story prepared."

With that, Kitty turned in a flourish and left to go talk with someone else, leaving Faith in a daze. The blood rushing in her ears drowned out the music, and she felt as if she might faint. Her eyes searched the room for Irvin, and in no time their gazes collided.

His gaze dropped to her lips. He shifted his stance and tugged on the waistband of his pants, drawing her attention to his groin. Her overactive imagination took over, and she pictured him slowly hardening until he was completely rigid and ready.

Ready for her.

Heat simmered across her skin, making her feel as if

she were on fire. She jerked her eyes upward, expecting to find a smirk on his face after catching her staring at his crotch. Instead, he gave her a smoldering look. He spoke to the people around him before coming her way.

She'd be a fool to turn that down, right? Nobody would dig into her life if she was only a one-night stand. Besides, she didn't want the fame, or the apartment in New York like a kept woman. One night was all she wanted. All she'd allow herself.

He stopped in front of her, his shoulders stiff and his brows drawn together. "Did Kitty say something to upset you?"

"No. Actually, she said something very interesting."

His brow quirked, and the barest hint of a smile graced his lips. "I'd like to hear it."

"She said you've spent the night staking your claim on me. That you've never looked at a woman the way you're looking at me, and that I should move my family to New York and be with you."

Her heart fluttered in her chest as she waited for his response. He would laugh, right? Scoff at Kitty's outrageous claim and tell her not to quit her day job. Instead, the heat between them sizzled and popped as he took a step closer and his eyes became serious.

"Kitty talks too much," he said.

"She's crazy. I knew she was crazy."

"She's accurate, as usual. Faith, I don't understand it, and I can't say that this is forever, but right now, at this moment, all I know is that I want more time with you. I don't want this weekend to end."

One night. That's all. One night. The words ran through her head like a mantra. "We don't know each other. This stuff doesn't happen for real."

"Then let's get to know each other." He took her

hand in his. The breeze carried his cologne to her, and the scent heated her insides.

"I don't know if we should."

"If I weren't Irvin Freeman the movie star and I was just a guy you'd met, would you say no?"

She couldn't lie. "I wouldn't."

"Then forget about who I am and how we met. Just trust that fate brought us together for a reason."

Before she could answer him, the moment was interrupted when someone yelled and jumped into the hot tub. The crowd cheered, and the music increased in tempo.

He glanced around, then turned back to her. "Let's get out of here."

"Where are we going?"

"My place."

Two simple words that held the power to change everything. If she said yes, she knew what would happen. If she said no, she'd regret it forever...

She exhaled the breath she held and whispered her answer.

Chapter 12

It wouldn't be very charming of him to pounce on Faith. Yet trying not to pounce on her was proving difficult, if not damned impossible. He wanted to take things slow, not scare her by ripping that dress from her body and making love to her long and hard. The problem was, there was no eloquent way to express what was going through him right now.

His driver could barely contain his shock when Irvin gave the order to go to his place. The place he didn't bring women was the first place he wanted to bring Faith. He didn't want their first time to be in a hotel room.

He wanted to taste every part of her. Have her wetness on his tongue, feel the hardness of her nipples between his lips and run his hands across every soft inch of her skin. And he wanted to do it all in his bed, then wake up in the morning with her curled up next to him.

She stopped as soon as they entered his flat. "The view is beautiful." Faith's voice, quiet and husky, nearly made him groan. She crossed the living area to the windows overlooking the city.

He didn't turn on the lamp; instead, he watched her from the doorway. Her body was a sexy silhouette against the city lights. Mostly hidden by the shadows as she was, he could make out only glimpses of her. A tantalizing peek at her elbow, a brief view of her face.

He cleared his throat. "Not as beautiful as you."

"Me being here pretty much assures you're going to get lucky. You don't have to toss on the flattery." He couldn't see it, but he heard the smile in her voice.

"I don't want you to change your mind," he teased.

"You don't have to worry about that. I know what I'm getting into."

He crossed the room to stand beside her. "What are you getting into?"

"A one-night stand with a movie star."

In the dim light, he could see the rapid rise and fall of her chest. He brushed the hair away from her neck and leaned down to kiss the soft skin below her ear.

"I'm not a movie star tonight."

"I know we said that, but I have to keep reminding myself that you are." Her breathless voice fired his blood. She leaned closer to him.

"Why?"

"Otherwise, I might start to believe this can be more."

He met her eyes. "It is more." He tilted his head toward the door leading to the balcony. "Come, let me show you the view from there."

He held out his hand for her and led her to the wide terrace overlooking the Hudson River. A concrete-and-glass guardrail ran along the entire west end of the apartment. The wind had picked up, the precursor of a forecast storm for the next day. Faith shivered and wrapped her arms around herself. He pressed a button at the outdoor bar that turned on a gas fireplace.

She gasped when the flames flickered, and she walked over to the warmth. She held out her hands, then looked around the outdoor space. "I bet you have amazing parties here."

He strolled over to stand beside her at the fireplace. In the twinkling firelight he admired the smoothness of her skin.

"Sometimes," he replied, "but nothing like the party we just left. I only invite a handful of friends to my apartment."

"So the after-party won't follow us here."

"No."

"Good." She nodded, then met his eyes.

The smell of her perfume wafted around him like a cloud of silk. Their eyes met and electric heat sparked.

To hell with not pouncing on her. He took her elbow in his hand and pulled her to him. She lifted her chin, then raised herself on her toes. It was all the invitation he needed.

The kiss started soft, but he couldn't keep it tame for long. With one hand he cupped her face; the other wrapped around her waist to press her body fully against him. It took a second to realize her hands were all over him. Rubbing his head, gripping his arms, clenching the sides of his shirt. Her soft moans punctuated the silence, and something deep inside him celebrated. He craved her desire more than he could have imagined.

As much as he loved kissing her, that wasn't his ultimate goal. He lifted his head to take in how good she looked in the moonlight. His mouth watered. He gently ran his hands up her arms, then around back to her zipper. He waited a second, giving her time to say no. She didn't.

He slowly unzipped the dress and pushed the straps off her shoulders and down her arms. The dress fell in a whisper of material to her feet. His heart thundered and his body trembled at the sight of her breasts in a red silk bra. The thin material clung to the protruding tips of her breasts. He would never forget how beautiful she looked.

He ran his fingers along the edge, then dipped one finger below the silk to brush the soft skin on the side of her breast. She pulled her lower lip between her teeth as the back of his finger traced closer to her nipple. Her small hands gripped his waist, pulling him closer. He watched as the peaks hardened even more.

He leaned forward to brush his lips across her neck, breathing in the sweetness of her perfume and something far more addictive that belonged just to her. He reached behind her to unfasten her bra, but in his urgency he pulled too hard and tore the material.

"My apologies."

"Unnecessary."

He lowered his head to kiss the chocolate tips of her breasts before finally sucking one deep into his mouth. Her sigh and moan were his rewards.

He let the swollen nipple slip from between his lips, giving himself a second to admire the glistening tip before turning his attention on the other. He wanted more.

She was actually doing this. It wasn't a fantasy, and he wasn't a figment of her imagination. There was no need to pinch herself, because the wonderful feel of his lips on her body was definitely real and better than anything she could have possibly imagined.

Her breathing staggered as he hooked his fingers in the edge of her panties and tugged them down, his strong hands caressing every inch of her legs along the way. The heat from his palms seared straight through the taut muscles of her thighs, making her wet and wanting.

When he disposed of her panties, Irvin leaned forward to kiss her softly. But they were way beyond soft kisses now. If she was going to do this, then she was going to get as much as she could out of it. The memories would need to last a lifetime. She grabbed the back of his head and kissed him harder.

The movement elicited a deep groan from him. His hot lips left her mouth to travel down her neck to her exposed breasts. Her head fell back, but her eyes remained open. She wanted to remember everything about this moment. The sound of their ragged breathing against the muted background noises of the city. The black velvet of the sky above their heads. The scratch of his beard against the tender skin of her breasts. She lowered her gaze to the top of Irvin's head, then bit her lower lip as she watched him kiss and suckle her breasts.

His tongue circled one dark peak, and she nearly gasped from the exquisite pleasure. She watched shamelessly as he savored her. He caught her watching him, grinned and gently bit the sensitive nub. Nothing in her life had turned her on as much as the sight of her dark nipple between his even white teeth.

"Do that again," she urged.

He did, playing and nipping until both tips protruded, hard and swollen from his attention. She floated in a haze of pleasure when he ran a finger across her wet core and nearly made her knees buckle.

He looked up. Excitement brightened his eyes before they burned hot with desire. "You're bare." He ran his fingers across her smooth outer lips as if checking to be sure.

"I don't like hair down there."

He made a sound, half moan, half growl, then stood back in order to stare at the treasure between her legs. She watched him, her breathing shallow, as he gently massaged the sensitive flesh. Her eyes closed when he softly pushed two fingers deep inside her. She forced them open again.

She pulled him back in for another kiss, this one more earth-shattering than the last with his long fingers sliding in and out of her.

Her body trembled. The need for release sent her closer to the edge. She reined it in. Not like this. She had to come with him inside her.

"Now, please, now," she said through clenched teeth.

"Not yet." He slipped his fingers out and spread her desire over the smooth lips of her sex. He gently cupped her in his hand before once again easing two fingers inside.

"Oh my God, Irvin," she said on a moan. Her body bucked. Pleasure exploded and popped across her nerve endings. Her inner walls clenched around the fingers buried deep inside her. She watched the satisfaction on his face as she came, the male pride clear in his features.

It took several seconds before she could form a coherent thought. Irvin kept his hand between her legs, which didn't help her regain her composure.

"I didn't want to come yet," she finally said.

"I plan to make you come over and over."

She frowned and shook her head. "That's the problem," she said in a shaky voice. "I can't come more than once. I've tried."

A delicious gleam came into his eyes. "You've never been my lover before."

Chapter 13

His *lover.* The word danced around her brain as he kissed her again and lifted her into his arms. *Lover* implied long-term. More than a quick weekend fling. No matter how much his use of the word thrilled her, she wouldn't get any crazy ideas. When the sun rose tomorrow they'd do the last appearance, giving his foundation the money he'd raised by offering himself up as a date. Then she'd get on a plane and go home.

But that was tomorrow. They still had tonight.

He carried her farther down the terrace. How he made his way when he continued to kiss her, she didn't know. She lost herself in his kiss, surrendering to the pleasure that came from being exactly where she wanted to be right now. She ached to tell him all the feelings that he'd awakened in her, all the longing that she felt for this to be more than one night, but she couldn't say those things out loud. But she could let him know by the way she touched him.

He took her through a door that led to his bedroom. Gently he lowered her beside the bed. Once her feet touched the floor, her hands went everywhere. Across his jaw to the tight curls at the back of his head. Over wide shoulders to push away the jacket of his suit. Then back to massage the hard muscles of his chest.

She eased him backward until he fell onto the bed.

"Come and get me." His voice wrapped around her and heightened her need.

She straddled his hips and lowered her head to kiss him again while his long fingers caressed her thighs. His pants rubbed against her exposed clit. She gasped and jerked away. It was not fair for him still to have on so many clothes. A sinful grin spread across his face as his hands ran up her legs to grip her bare behind and pull her firmly against his cock.

"Is that what you want?" He lifted his hips again.

She moaned. "Yes."

"Are you going to come for me again?" His hands cupped her breasts.

"I'm damn sure gonna try."

"Good, because I damn sure want to make you come several times before the sun rises." He grasped her thighs and pinned her legs with a steady strength while slowly lifting and lowering his hips beneath her.

Her pleasure mounted with each movement. Her hands became unsteady, her breathing more labored. Her eyes flicked to his dark eyes intently studying her. He looked ready to devour her.

She felt suddenly self-conscious, and her hands shook. She wasn't a vixen. Why had she pushed him onto the bed and jumped on him as if she were used to taking control? This man had sex with the finest women in the world. Her attempts were probably laughable.

She fumbled with removing his tie and unbuttoning his shirt. It should have taken seconds but felt like forever. With a deep breath, she raised her gaze to his. The tenderness she saw there reached far into her heart and banished all of her nervousness. He took her cheek in his hand and lowered her head for a kiss. It was softer, slower than before.

"I could watch you undress me all night," he said against her lips.

"I thought I would take all night."

"Then I could do this all night," he said, raising his hips again to rub against her wet center.

She moaned and tugged at the waistband of his pants. It didn't take nearly as long to get them undone. She gasped with pleasure as he lifted up to push them past his waist.

The weight of his erection bounced against her wetness. She mirrored his hip rotation to enjoy the wonderful sensation of his thickness against her.

"You feel so good," he said against her lips. "So damn good."

He swiftly wrapped his arms around her and flipped her onto the bed. They became a tangle of arms and legs. Soft kisses, caresses and words she wouldn't remember as they explored each other's bodies. As if they both realized what was happening between them was special, they took their time. Her body turned into one large nerve, tingling and tight with the need to explode. Her heart fell deeper and deeper for him with each passing second.

No other experience she'd ever had compared with what he was doing to her. She doubted it could be better, until he slid his body down and settled between her legs.

Through a cloud of desire she rose up on her elbows and stared at the slow plunder of his fingers inside her body. He trailed his tongue from her neck all the way to her waist and below. She froze with anticipation and nervousness. Would he really? He licked his lips. Oh, God, yes, he would. He slowly ran his tongue across the erect nub at the center of her sex.

She watched him, her vision blurring as he loved her body. Her moans were matched by his. It was one thing to have him kiss her this way, another to know he enjoyed it as much as she. Her desire built inside her, rising higher and higher until she knew he was going to prove her a liar. She was going to climax again.

But she wanted all of him, inside her, when she did.

She gripped his shoulder and tried to pull him up. She saw the reluctance in his eyes as he lifted away from her body. He met her eyes, then froze, a look she didn't recognize on his features.

"I can't let you go."

The words shattered any hope she had of not falling in love with him. She would be his forever. Even if he was hers for only tonight. She shoved the bittersweet thought aside.

She spread her arms and he came to her. She barely registered that he pulled a condom from the nightstand and put it on. Or that somehow in their twisting and turning, the duvet had come off the bed and they were lying on a tangle of sheets. The only thing that registered in her mind was the intense pleasure of them becoming one.

She took in everything. The weight of his body pressed against her. The way his hands gripped her hips and ran up and down her sides and across her cheek. He touched and moved against her as if she were precious, fragile. When he wasn't kissing her, his eyes never left hers. It was more than sex. It was a connection that she would cherish long after the night was over and they both moved on.

As her climax built, his breathing changed. His eyes grew urgent. His thrusts came faster, deeper, until she couldn't hold back. She let herself go, and the orgasm crashed into her like a freight train. Her entire body shook with the force of it. She felt it everywhere: skin, hair, toes and lungs. Every part of her reacted to the beauty of her and Irvin.

He held her afterward. Not just a simple arm around her shoulders. No, he pulled her back against his chest, one arm around her waist so his hand could cup her breast, and squeezed her tight. She was actually spooning with Irvin Freeman. But it was more than that. He had erased any thoughts of him being the movie star and made her see only the guy she was falling in love with.

Tears threatened. It would all end in less than twenty-four hours.

"Are you awake?" he asked and kissed her shoulder.

She closed her eyes to stop the tears and nodded. "Isn't it the guy who falls asleep afterward?"

His chuckle vibrated across her skin. "That was like a shot of adrenaline."

"It was pretty powerful," she said with a smile.

"The sounds you make," he said in a deep, sexy voice. He kneaded her breast in his hand and pushed the hair away from her ear to gently kiss it. "A guy could get used to hearing that."

A girl could get used to having someone bring out those sounds. Who was she kidding? After only one time, she couldn't imagine making love like that with anyone else. He'd always be in her heart. She knew that now. Her sexual partners were few, which meant Irvin Freeman would be a part of her for the rest of her life.

And he'd move on and forget her. Her heart stung

with the thought. A dozen wasps in her chest couldn't have inflicted more pain. She wanted more, needed more to take with her.

"Tell me about your family," she said.

His movements on her breast stopped, and his body tightened next to her. She held her breath as she waited. There wasn't much about his family life in the media. All she knew was what he'd mentioned earlier in the day. Now, knowing she'd go home with only a night of sex to remember, she wanted to know. Wanted to see a part of him that few others would.

He tugged on her shoulder until she lay on her back. Leaning up on an elbow, he stared down at her.

"Only if you'll tell me what you're hiding."

"I'm not hiding anything." Her voice didn't conceal her panic.

"Something happened with your sister. Tell me about that."

She frowned, not wanting to air her family's dirty laundry. Even to Irvin. It had been so hard, so humiliating to have her twin do that to their parents. He didn't press, not verbally, anyway. But his eyes never left hers. She understood what he was doing. If she was going to probe, then so would he.

"After my mama got sick, Love—my sister—stole everything."

"What do you mean?"

"I mean everything. She cleaned out both of my parents' bank accounts. Took any valuable jewelry they had and a few antique pieces that had been in our family for years. It ruined any chances they had for a comfortable retirement—" she sighed and pressed her palm to her forehead "—or for paying the medical bills for Mama's recovery."

"Do you know why?"

Anger made Faith grip the sheet. "My sister is a drug addict. She started when we were in high school. She'd stolen from us before, but it was always small. A couple hundred bucks here or there. Then she'd disappear for a while or try to clean up, only to start over. This time she went too far. Mama was still in the hospital, barely twelve hours past her stroke, when Love took everything."

"It sounds like something bad happened."

"Something bad did happen."

"I mean to your sister. She had to have been desperate."

Faith didn't want to hear anything resembling sympathy for her sister. She scooted away and sat up on the bed. She pulled her knees up and rested her elbows on them. "I would never be desperate enough to take everything from our parents."

"Are you sure she wasn't in trouble?"

Faith sighed and stared out of the glass balcony doors at the twinkling skyline. It was well past midnight. Back home everything would be dark; here everything still shone brightly.

"If she were in that much trouble, she should have come to me. I wouldn't have liked it, but I would have helped her. Despite her years of addiction, I wanted her to get better. But her doing that to Mama and Daddy… That was my last straw."

Irvin moved to sit up beside her. "You still pay for her rehab."

"Mama begged me to." She took a deep breath. "And she's my twin. I can't stop hoping, just a little, that she'll get better."

"People in desperate situations don't realize that all they need to do is ask for help."

"Asking for help is easier than hurting people you love."

"Have you ever been desperate?"

The way he asked made her turn to him. He too looked out at the skyline, with a faraway look in his eye.

"Have you?" she asked.

"I've watched people in desperate situations try to handle it themselves."

"Your family?"

He nodded. "My parents. My father struggled with alcoholism. Most days he was tolerable. Drunk, but tolerable."

"And on other days?"

A frown stained his features. "On other days he was a monster. Violent, angry and uncontrollable. When I begged my mother to get help, she always refused. She preferred to hide it." He gave Faith a sad half smile. "My mother actually came from a good family. Her father was a top barrister, her mother a well-respected professor."

"I've heard that about you," Faith said.

"Because her family claimed me after I became famous. When my mother met and fell for my father, they disowned her. Said she was making a mistake." He gave a humorless laugh and tugged on the sheet. "Funny how right they were. Still, she wouldn't give them the satisfaction. She became an expert at hiding my dad's problem and our bruises. I became an expert at pretending to be a happy child whose father wasn't an alcoholic. I guess that's why acting came so naturally to me."

Faith flinched, hurting for him and an upbringing she couldn't fathom. Hesitantly she reached over to place her hand on his back. He took her other hand in his.

"What happened?"

"My father got smashed one night and drove home. He killed an entire family." He nodded when Faith gasped. "Can't hide four dead bodies. So, off he went to jail. I couldn't forgive him, but my mother decided to be there for him."

"What did you do?"

"I stopped trying to protect her. I left and came to the States. Until then, I'd turned down every opportunity to walk away. I would refuse to spend the night at friends' flats so I could take the blows meant for her when he became violent. I turned down several scholarships, all to protect my mother. It wasn't until he killed a family that I realized I couldn't save people from themselves. I could only save myself from them."

"How did your parents die?"

He turned to look at her. "My father got hold of some rubbing alcohol six months after being in jail and drank too much of it. He died not long after I moved away. I tried to get my mother to move over here, but she refused. So I sent her money. Got her a fancy flat when I made it big, and would visit at least twice a year. By then, her family was ready to take her back into their fold. She got sick a few years back. Meningitis. It took her quickly."

Faith didn't say anything. Instead, she leaned over and kissed his shoulder. He wrapped his arm around her and pressed a kiss to her temple. When he lifted his head, she tilted hers back to stare at him. He was so handsome. But before the weekend, he'd seemed like a dream. This outrageously fine, untouchable man that hovered in the fantasy world of Hollywood. Now he seemed real.

"Make love to me again," she whispered.

"As if I weren't already planning to do that." He

kissed her and eased her back into the pillows. Faith let the sadness of their revelations melt away as their bodies came together.

Chapter 14

"It was a pleasure to help raise funds for such a fantastic mission. I've always believed that the small actions people take toward a cause add up to tremendous results. And though it may seem as if the biggest winner here is Faith, we all know that the winners are the people who will benefit from the funds we raised."

Cameras flashed, and the large group standing behind the podium all clapped. They were in the lobby of the headquarters of Irvin's foundation, Starting Over. Irvin was giving his speech before he presented the check for the money raised by this campaign. Standing behind him, Faith couldn't stop herself from staring at him. The man was devastating in a dark brown suit and tan silk tie. She'd overheard the appreciative gasps of the women when he'd walked into the room and flashed that smile. Instead of being jealous, she'd felt a little cocky. They had connected last night, if only briefly. She had something with Irvin that no other woman did.

For now.

She blinked and pressed a hand to the side of her head to push the thought away. The future didn't matter. What mattered was this exact second in her life. The last few moments she had with him. She needed to drink it all in. In a few short hours she'd be back on a plane on her way home.

Kitty treated her as more than just the weekend prop. The publicist hadn't seemed surprised to find Faith at Irvin's apartment that morning. In fact, she'd brought Faith's outfit for the presentation, a cute sleeveless coral dress that flared into an A-line skirt above her knees. She still barked orders and referred to the itinerary, but now she insisted that someone get Faith some water because she looked thirsty. And ordered one of the members of her crew to go out for cupcakes when Faith made an offhand comment about wanting another like she'd had with Irvin the other night.

Faith guessed the change was Kitty's assumption that Faith was Irvin's new woman. Though the thought flattered her, it also made her uneasy. She didn't want people fetching her water or running out for cupcakes on Kitty's command. She wanted only Irvin. But Irvin came with all that, and she wasn't sure she was up for the constant scrutiny.

The applause died down and Irvin spoke again. "I always knew I had the best fans in the world. But half a million dollars for my foundation was more than I could imagine they would raise. If I'd known offering myself up as a prize would raise so much, I would have done it a lot sooner."

That got a laugh out of the crowd. "Especially if I'd known the winner would be so wonderful."

He nailed Faith with a hot stare that whipped up

memories of the night before. The weight of his body on top of her, his hands caressing her breasts. He licked his lips, and her face burned with the memory of the way he'd licked her so thoroughly. Her passion ignited with such strength, she was surprised the hairs on her arms didn't catch fire.

She struggled to take in a breath.

"Irvin," one of the reporters at the press conference called out, breaking the moment. "Since this was so successful, will you do this again?"

Time stood still as she waited on the answer. A yes meant she was easily replaceable. A no meant... Well, it didn't mean forever with him, but it also didn't mean he was eager to have another woman spend the weekend with him.

"No," he said. "I hope to find other ways to raise funds."

A few reporters turned her way, and she fought not to squirm. After several more questions, Irvin presented the check to the chairman of the board and shook hands with him, and they posed for pictures. Then she noticed Irvin's artist friend Carl was looking at her, too, and smiling. He looked completely different in a pair of faded jeans and a button-down red-and-blue-striped shirt.

"Freeman put me on the list," he said when she walked over to shake his hand. "He's the only one left who has any hope I'll shake this thing."

"I have hope, too," she said, even more touched by Irvin's assistance to the man after his confession about his own father the night before.

"I'm almost done with your drawing. I'll make sure Freeman gets it to you." Carl gave her a knowing grin. "I'm sure he'll be in touch."

Faith wished more than anything that were the case.

After the press conference, a small group waited in the boardroom until the media cleared out. The foundation's chairman came over. "I bet you've had an exciting weekend."

"I have," Faith said with a smile.

"It's going to be hard to go home after this, huh?"

Painful was more like it. Still, she kept the smile on her face and nodded. "I'll manage. Besides, I'm looking forward to getting back. My parents are sick, and I'm their caretaker."

The chairman patted her on the arm. "Good for you."

It was an odd statement, but before Faith could comment, someone clasped her shoulder.

"Are you ready?" Kitty asked. "We've got to leave in order to get to the airport on time."

Faith's heart rate sprang into rocket speed. Already? The weekend would end just that quickly.

"Is it time?" She hated that her voice wavered with the question.

"Past time, really. But it took longer to clear the room than expected. Say your goodbyes and we'll be going."

Kitty rushed over to one of the members of her team. Faith's world tilted on its axis. How could she possibly say goodbye adequately? Had she overreacted and read too much into the weekend than there really was? She hadn't asked Irvin the details of her departure today because she'd known it was their last day together and she didn't want to spoil it, but she'd hoped for something other than an order from Kitty to say her goodbyes.

And where was Irvin?

She looked across the room to where Kitty had walked and she found him. He hadn't come to her after the press conference had ended. When they'd come in here, he'd talked to other people on the board. Was it because he didn't want to be the one to push her onto the plane?

Well, she would make it easy for him.

She hurried out of the boardroom and down the end of the empty hall. She stood in front of the window and stared out at the city, gray and damp with a rainstorm. She didn't want this life, but the thought of leaving made her throat tighten.

"Faith." Irvin's concerned voice came from behind her. "You all right?"

"Yeah… I just needed a second before I said my goodbyes."

"It should be easy," he said. Her back was to him, but she heard the humor in his voice.

She clenched her fists and glared out the window at the dreary landscape. "I guess it would be easy for you. A guy with your history must not have any trouble saying goodbye the next day."

"A guy with my history." All humor left his tone. "What's that supposed to mean?"

"I'm sure you've had your share of weekend flings. I know that what we did here isn't special."

In the reflection in the window, she watched him come closer. He crossed his arms, but she couldn't make out the expression on his face. "Where is this coming from, Faith?"

"You date a lot of women."

"Dating a lot of women doesn't mean I sleep with a lot of women."

"Come on, Irvin."

"Gossips like to link my name to different women, but it doesn't mean that it's true." He took her elbow in his hand and spun her to face him.

The hurt and anger in his expression took her breath

away. "What they report is nothing more than rumors. Despite what most of the world believes, I'm not sleeping with a new woman every night."

Her neck and cheeks prickled with heat. She shifted her eyes away from his. "I'm sorry. I didn't…"

"Let me guess. You didn't mean it?" He let her go and took a step back. "I thought last night meant something."

"It did. It does. I didn't want to come to New York, and I really didn't want to be another easy groupie that fell for you. But you turned out to be funny, and nice, and so sweet and considerate. And something clicks when I'm with you. Something that makes me want more than I can say." She met his eyes and felt her feelings for him rise up in her heart. "Then you kissed me and made love to me. It was like a dream come true. More than anything I ever could have imagined, and it touched something that I really didn't want you to touch."

The tension left his body, replaced by a look that was both nervous and unsure, as he came to her.

"Faith, I enjoyed this weekend with you. I didn't expect us to end up like this. It just happened."

"I know. I'm sorry. It's just that…this weekend doesn't mean as much to you as it does me. Okay, you don't sleep with a lot of women. I'll give you that. But by tomorrow, I'll be nothing more than the woman you had sex with one weekend after she won a date with you in a raffle. And right now, I need to remind myself of that."

He brushed the back of his hand across her face. "You're determined to believe that this isn't really happening between us. If you keep it up, I'm going to be insulted. I'm not letting this end. This is just beginning."

Her hands fell to her sides. "But Kitty told me to say my goodbyes."

"Yes, to the people here at the foundation. Not to me. You wouldn't really think I'd let her brush you off like that." He frowned, then held up a hand. "Never mind. What you said earlier means you would think that."

She tried not to get her hopes up, not when they still had an insurmountable problem. "How could we possibly make it work? I can't just leave my parents behind and move to New York."

"I wouldn't expect you to." He came close and took her hands in his. "But just because you're going home doesn't mean we're through."

"I've done long distance before. It didn't end very well."

"I'm not some prat who'll break up with you for taking care of your family."

"It wasn't just my family," she said, trying not to lose herself in the warmth of his eyes and smile. Long distance with her ex was one thing, but long distance with a man like Irvin seemed downright impossible. "My ex needed someone to fit his image. You're the same. You're Irvin Freeman. You're supposed to be with someone like Selena, not a country nurse."

"Says who? The gossip columnists? I'm supposed to be with the person I choose to be with." He tugged her hands to bring her forward. "And I chose you."

The look, his cologne, the voice… It all drew her in. Made her believe and trust that it could work. Still… "I'm serious, Irvin. It's going to be hard. This weekend was great, but it won't be like this always."

"I'm serious, too, Faith. I'll come see you in South Carolina. On your weekends off, you can visit me. I'll even pay for your family to come with you or for a live-in nurse to help out so the burden isn't all on you."

"I can't let you do that." She turned away.

He placed a hand on her chin and gently turned her back to him. "I want to. I told you once that I believe in fate. It brought us together, and I'm not willing to let go of what we started here just because we don't live in the same state."

"You make it sound so easy," she said.

"It may not be easy, but it's worth it."

He smiled, and her heart did a squat jump in her chest. Her breathing hitched as he lowered his head to kiss her.

"Not now, you two." Kitty's voice broke in right before Irvin's lips touched Faith's. "The plane is waiting."

Disappointment like she'd never experienced in her life weighed on her chest. "You've got to tell her to stop interrupting our kisses," she said.

Irvin grinned. "I think she has internal radar that lets her know I'm about to put her behind schedule."

"The time to go came so soon," she whispered.

"Saying goodbye is always the hardest part," Irvin whispered. He stepped back and took her hand in his. "That's why I'm going to make our first one special."

The look on Faith's face when she realized he was flying her back on a private jet made him happier than any flattering review for one of his movies. Her grin was more impressive than the luxurious furnishings.

"You own a jet, too?" she said, spinning around and taking in their surroundings.

"Sorry to disappoint you, but no. I don't mind traveling commercially and would rather put my money in real estate. This is my friend Dante's plane."

"I guess that makes sense. It looks more like him than you."

He chuckled and glanced around at the dark wood with matching Italian leather furniture, a fully stocked bar and a sixty-inch television in the main cabin.

"What makes it look more like him than me?"

"You're not as flashy."

He sat on one of the leather seats and pulled her down on his lap. Her laughter and warm curves lit a fire in his body that only grew hotter when he kissed her.

Still, he wondered how they would make this relationship work. For all of his talk back at the foundation, he was concerned about what would happen when they parted. As for him, he was used to long-distance relationships. The last woman he'd dated was also an actor, and they frequently were in different cities, or countries, depending on their schedules. When he was with a woman exclusively, he was faithful. He didn't have time to invite drama into his life. So he wasn't worried about his needs. He was worried about how Faith would deal with it. It was one thing to trust him when they were together, another when they were apart and the media began circulating rumors about him. The last thing he wanted was for his celebrity status to make her doubt him.

So he planned to make sure that she knew exactly how much he wanted her before he left her and every time they got together.

The flight crew interrupted their kiss to ask them to put on seat belts for takeoff.

"This is the worst part," Faith said. She clutched the arms of the chair.

"It'll be over before you know it."

She frowned. "And I'll be home before we know it. It's only a two-hour flight." She glanced at him from her seat, which she'd regretfully had to move into for take-off. "How long will you stay? I know you're supposed to be in Canada tomorrow."

"I'd hoped to stay the night."

"As much as I would love that, my parents might think it's weird for me to bring you home. And I don't think they'd approve of you sleeping in my bed."

"Prudish?"

"Not exactly. But take away your movie-star status again and you're a man I met two days ago, and you're spending the night with me already."

He winced and grinned. "It does sound like we've rushed into it."

"It does."

"So I won't spend the night, but I will stay in town. And come see you before I go in the morning."

"And I can spend some time with you at your hotel tonight. Though it won't be as luxurious as you're used to."

"With you in the bed, it doesn't matter."

The plane sped up on the runway then, and her grip tightened on the chair. He placed his hand on hers. Several minutes later, the flight attendant came by and let them know they could remove their seat belts. He also brought chilled champagne with an assortment of fruits and cheeses.

Faith didn't take off her seat belt.

"You can remove that," Irvin said with a smile.

"I know, but it just makes me feel safer."

"You don't like flying, I gather."

"It's a necessary thing. I don't hate it, but it's not fun, either."

He raised a brow. "You could find fun ways to distract yourself."

"I've tried them all. Reading, listening to music, watching a movie. Nothing distracts me enough."

"You know if we plummet to the earth, wearing a seat belt won't keep you alive."

She cut her eyes at him. "You're not helping."

He uncorked the champagne and poured her a glass. She raised an eyebrow when he put the bottle back into the ice.

"You don't want any?"

He shrugged. "I only have one drink per day."

"Why?"

"To avoid becoming like my father. When I first came to New York, it was easy to party and drink until the sun rose. I stumbled in one night after doing just that, looked in the mirror and froze. I looked exactly like him. It scared the life out of me."

She put her glass down and placed her hand on his. "To do what he did meant he didn't have your goodness in his heart. I can't imagine you becoming like him."

Her confidence warmed him more than any stage light ever had. "I appreciate that, more than I can say."

"If you're not drinking then I'm not," she said.

"Which means you still need a distraction."

Her hair was pulled back into a neat chignon. Between the hair and the dress she'd worn to the press conference, she looked like the cool and collected woman in the picture Kitty had first shown him. He wanted the warm and mussed woman that moaned his name in that sexy Southern accent of hers.

He popped off his seat belt and stood over her. "I'm about to help." He unhooked her seat belt and pulled her from the chair.

The second her soft curves met his hard muscles,

need stirred in his groin to have her naked against him once again.

"How are you going to help?" Her voice became husky and her eyes softened.

"Follow me." He took her hand and led her through a door beside the television to a separate bedroom. It was decorated in the same dark colors, along with a king-size bed with a chocolate duvet.

"You want me to take a nap?" she asked with a teasing smile.

"I want you in that bed." He stood behind her and slowly unzipped the back of her dress. "But not for a nap."

"I don't know. Sleeping is usually how I distract myself while flying." She teased him, but he could hear the desire in her voice.

He pushed the dress off her shoulders, then stepped back just enough to take in all of her wonderful curves from the back. He felt himself grow harder as his gaze fell on the skimpy black panties and the cuff of her butt beneath the edges.

"I'm about to show you a new way to enjoy a flight." He put his hand on her waist and pulled her against him. He pressed his cock into her backside. "How about that?"

Her head fell back. He looked down her body at her wonderful breasts in the sexy bra and all that silky brown skin. He wanted to taste every inch of her.

He brought his hand up to cup her breast, using his finger to trace the hardened nipple through the lace. She moaned and rubbed against him.

"Is that my answer?" he said against her ear.

She nodded, and he nipped at the bottom of her earlobe. His other hand dived past the waistband of her panties to her desire-slickened sex. His knees trembled as he caressed the smooth skin with his fingers. She was already wet and swollen. Ready for him. He ran his fingers against her dewy treasure before sinking his middle finger inside. Her walls clenched around him, and he groaned.

"When you touch me like that," she panted, "it makes me want to do things."

He slipped his finger out and dived back in. "What things?"

She turned in his arms. The smile she gave him turned his penis into granite. He was crazy about this woman.

"Why don't I show you?" she asked.

She lowered to her knees, tugging on the waistband of his pants as she went down. Each pull ignited an urgency inside him until her warm hand clasped him in her grip. The first press of her lips against him nearly toppled him down. When her hot mouth closed around him, he thought he would explode right then. He gripped her head, then had to force himself to loosen his hold. But it was difficult when her tongue did things to him he would never forget. The memories of this encounter would keep him awake and hard every night they were separated.

He felt his climax coming and pulled her up before it could arrive. Lifting her into his arms, he hurried across the room and fell onto the bed with her. His mouth didn't break from hers the entire time. It took only a few seconds to remove his clothes, and he would owe her another pair of undergarments because he tore her panties in his urgency to get them off.

He lowered between her legs and returned her favor. He loved the taste of her. And her bare lower lips gave him unblocked access to every nook and crevice.

"Irvin, yes. Please. Don't stop" were the words she said over and over.

"I'm not stopping until we both can't walk," he said against her sweetness.

Lifting away from this feast, he got a condom from his pants pocket, put it on and sank deeply into her body. Her legs wrapped tightly around his waist. Her hips rose to meet his thrust for thrust. She twisted and he moved with her; she begged for more and he gave her more. He didn't know if it was turbulence or the emotions Faith awakened in him, but his body shook. And when he followed her over the edge, he realized that despite knowing her only a few days, he was quickly falling in love with Faith Logan.

Chapter 15

Faith wished she could stop herself from smiling like the Cheshire Cat in *Alice in Wonderland*, but her mouth refused to cooperate. As the plane landed and Irvin continued to rub his thumb gently back and forth across the back of her hand in his, she felt like Alice. She'd fallen into a wonderful parallel universe or something. If it weren't for the delicious ache between her legs, she wouldn't believe this was happening. That she'd not only made love on a private jet, but that she was falling in love.

She almost hated to admit that she was falling in love with him. Insecurities tried to creep in, but every time he smiled at her, and she remembered how things were when they were alone, she pushed her doubts away.

They got off the plane at the private airstrip. She'd been there several times as a child. The owner, Gary Baker, used to invite the community over during the summer for trips in his small one-engine plane around the county. An event that turned into a minifair with game booths, food vendors and even a live band. He'd stopped it several years ago after his wife passed away.

"Hi, Gary," Faith said when they got off the plane.

Gary's dark eyes twinkled in his wrinkled face, and he opened his arms wide to give her a hug.

"As soon as they told me you were flying in, I had to come down and say hello," Gary said.

"How did you know I was on the plane?"

Gary pulled back and eyed Irvin over her shoulder. "You're the only one in town who won a weekend with a movie star. They told me Irvin Freeman needed it, so I put two and two together."

Irvin walked up and held out his hand. "Thank you very much for allowing us to use your strip. It was quite the surprise to find out there was a private airstrip here. I didn't think we'd get closer than Greenville."

"Well, that's what you get for thinking," Gary said with a wide grin on his face.

"I guess you're right," Irvin said, returning Gary's grin.

"It may not be here for long," Gary said, looking around at the empty bay that once held his plane. "I'm thinking of selling. Might move closer to town. Kinda quiet and lonely out here all by myself."

Gary and his late wife had loved each other deeply. It had been obvious whenever the two were around. He was still his normal good-natured self, but his smile had definitely dimmed in the years since she passed.

"You can always come have dinner with me and my parents," Faith offered.

"I would," Gary said, "if you were ever off work."

He looked to Irvin. "I'm so glad she won that trip. This woman deserves to get out and have a good time."

"I hope to give her a lot of good times in the future," Irvin said, taking her hand in his again. She'd never realized how much she loved holding hands with a man until she'd met Irvin.

"I take that to mean you'll be around for a while," Gary said.

"As long as she'll have me."

Gary nodded. "Good deal."

After a few more minutes chatting with Gary, they loaded up the back of the car Irvin had reserved for them and made their way to her parents' house.

During the ride she answered his questions about the town. But her anxiety grew with each mile. Two years of not bringing a man home and she was arriving with one after only a few short days. And not just any man. A movie star. Her parents were going to think she was crazy, or stupid, or both. Mama had told her to have fun, not fall head over heels. And she definitely hadn't told her to bring him home and say she was about to turn their lives upside down by dating someone so famous.

"We're here, cutie," Irvin said.

Faith jumped at his voice. She hadn't realized they'd stopped. She swallowed hard and turned to Irvin. "They're really nice...normally."

"Normally? Should I expect this to be an abnormal visit?"

"What do you think?"

He smiled, that damn wonderful heart-melting smile of his, then leaned over and kissed her cheek. "Just the first round of scrutiny in our relationship."

"I'd rather face the paparazzi," she said.

When the driver opened the door, she saw her mama

and daddy sitting on the front porch. Their smiles brightened when she got out of the car. Those smiles drifted into looks of confusion when Irvin got out, but then, like good Southern folk, they quickly pasted on a welcoming grin. Only Faith recognized they weren't very sincere.

"Hey, Mama and Daddy," Faith said after she and Irvin crossed the lawn to the front porch.

"Faith, it's good to see you," her mama said, her Southern accent full of questions.

She hugged her daddy first, then bent down to hug her mama.

"And you brought a visitor." Her daddy held out his hand to Irvin. "Jimmy Logan."

"Irvin Freeman." Irvin shook her dad's outstretched hand.

"I didn't know the prize included a personal return home by Irvin Freeman," her mama said.

Irvin shook her hand next. His thousand-watt smile turned on full blast her mama's way. Virginia wasn't immune. She shifted in her chair and patted the bun at the back of her head.

"It didn't originally, but I wasn't ready to say goodbye," Irvin said. He took a step closer to Faith and wrapped her hand in his.

Virginia and Jimmy looked at their entwined hands, then at each other.

"Just why weren't you ready to say goodbye?" her dad asked.

"Faith and I got along very well in New York," Irvin said.

"How well?" Virginia asked. She leaned her elbow on the arm of the chair and nailed him with a sweet smile laced with a bit of caution that seemed to say *mess up if you want to.*

Irvin cleared his throat and threw Faith a glance. She'd tried to warn him.

"Well enough for me to recognize that I'd like to spend more time with her," he said.

Jimmy crossed his arms. "Time doing what?"

"Dating. We've decided to start dating," Irvin answered quickly.

"Aren't you dating that actress Selena Jones?" her mama fired off next.

"No, ma'am. Selena and I are just friends."

Again her parents exchanged looks. She didn't know if it was the *ma'am* or the sincerity in his voice, but they both nodded and turned genuine welcoming smiles in his direction.

"Well, why didn't you say so?" Virginia asked. "Come on in. I just made some sweet tea."

Virginia maneuvered her chair around with her husband's help, and they went inside. Irvin wiped his brow and gave Faith a grin.

"What did I say that won them over?"

She shook her head. "I don't know if it was your smile or that sexy accent of yours."

"I doubt either would work on your father," he said with a grin.

They followed her parents into the cool interior of the house. The front door opened directly into the living room. Irvin stopped and looked around. She bit her lip as she watched him. Their house was clean and homey, but nowhere near as fashionable or spotless as his New York condo.

"I love it," he said.

"Really?"

"Yes, it feels like a home," he said. "I haven't been

in a real home in…" He paused and a sad look crossed his features.

His childhood home wouldn't have felt like one, not the way he described it. He might never have been in one. He'd left London and come straight to America and the life he lived now.

"Then we'll be sure to make you feel at home," Virginia said from the end of the hall. "Come on down. I made biscuits this morning."

The wistful look left Irvin's face, replaced with his smile. "I thought biscuits were a breakfast food," he said, glancing at his watch. "It's well past noon."

"It's never a bad time of day for biscuits and molasses," her mama said. "Faith, haven't you told him anything?"

They laughed and followed Virginia down the hall.

"We're really going to a place called Hole in the Wall?" Irvin asked Faith.

They were back in the car, heading out for a night on the town her parents insisted they have. He'd known he was going to like Virginia Logan the second she'd quickly broken his melancholy in her living room. He'd known his upbringing wasn't the happiest and had thought he'd come to grips with that. But seeing the Logans' living room with hand-stitched quilts, family pictures on the walls and old trophies had done something to him. Despite the problems with Faith's sister, her pictures were still there. A testament to the fact that the family, at one time, had loved each other.

"Yes," Faith said. She leaned against his side, his arm around her shoulders. She'd insisted that they didn't need to dress up and was wearing jean shorts and a dark blue blouse. He didn't think he'd like anything better than the skimpy dress she'd worn to the club, but he loved this simple outfit. It was how she'd looked when he'd first seen her. Without all the glamour they'd thrown on her for the weekend. It enhanced her sexiness more than any other outfit he'd seen her in.

"It's named after the Mel Waiters song."

"I don't think I've ever heard that one."

She lifted her head and looked at him as if he'd spoken in tongues. "You haven't heard the song? It's a classic. Don't worry. It's guaranteed they'll play it. You've got to get up and do the two-step when it comes on."

"I don't know that dance, either," he said with a laugh.

"It's as easy as it sounds," she said, leaning her head back on his shoulder. "Are you sure you're okay with doing this? It's not like the fancy nightclubs you're used to in New York, but the people here are friendly. And if you don't want to be bothered with autographs and such, they'll leave you alone."

"That stuff doesn't bother me," he said as he kissed the top of her head. "Besides, your father said this is the best hangout in all of Laurel County."

"It's the only hangout," she said with a chuckle.

They arrived a few minutes later, and Irvin had to admit the place lived up to the name. It was a large wooden building with Hole in the Wall painted on the front. The dirt parking area was full of cars, and more lined the dirt road.

"Busy place," he said.

"You should see it on Saturday night," Faith said.

"Do you come here often?"

She shook her head. "No. When I'm off I try to spend time at home with Mama and Daddy. But my friend Marie comes a lot. Her truck's right over there." She pointed to a dark truck parked a few cars over. "I guess you'll get to meet all the important people in my life today."

The idea sent an unfamiliar warmth through his chest. He wanted to know the people important to her.

They entered the club, if you'd call it that. Wooden tables and chairs crowded the floor. Cigarette smoke hung in the air, along with the smell of frying food. People talked and laughed all over the place and congregated on a small dance area next to an old piano. The stereo and speakers on top of the piano were so big he was surprised the instrument could support the weight.

This was a far cry from the clubs Kitty dragged him out to.

"Faith!" A woman's yell cut through the noise and music. A woman with dark brown skin and short black hair jumped up from a nearby table and ran over. She grabbed Faith into a huge hug. "When did you get home?"

"Today," Faith said.

"What? Why didn't you call me? You know I want to hear all of the juicy details."

Faith laughed. "That's why I brought the details with me." She turned to Irvin. "Irvin, meet my best friend, Marie."

Marie's mouth dropped open. Then a sly smile spread across her full lips. "You brought him home," she said, slapping the side of Faith's arm. "What did you do up there, girl?"

"She completely bewitched me," Irvin said, pulling Faith to his side.

"Oh my word, that accent," Marie said, fanning herself.

"I'm more of a fan of her accent," Irvin said with a grin.

Faith nudged him with her elbow. "Stop. Everyone

in New York kept asking where I was from the second
I opened my mouth. Like they've never heard a South-
erner speak before. I must sound terrible."

"You sound wonderful," he said, kissing her cheek.

"I can't believe it," Marie said with a grin. "Hey,
everyone, Faith is back, and she brought one hell of a
souvenir."

That called up a round of well wishes, and several
people came over to meet him and shake his hand. All
of them told Faith they were glad she'd had a good time
and that she deserved to get out more. She'd told him
that her life since coming home was devoted to taking
care of her parents, and now their words proved it. He
didn't know how, or if she'd even want his help, but he
was going to find a way to bring fun and relaxation
back into her life.

True to Faith's word, after the crowd greeted him,
they went back to doing their own things. One woman
had even told him she thought his last movie could have
been better, but she didn't blame him for the funky ending. He'd laughed. No one in New York dared tell him
his movies weren't good, and he agreed the ending
wasn't the best.

"Are you ready to have a good time?" Faith asked
him.

"Are you ready to show me a good time?"

"Just you wait and see, city boy," she said, her sexy
accent filling him with heat. "I took tomorrow off already, so I can stay out all night."

They found a table near the bar. Marie and her boyfriend joined them. He heard the song the place was
named after, and he learned the two-step. The song
talked about whiskey and chicken wings, so he took his
one drink of the day to pay homage to the lyrics before

switching to soda. By the end of the night, he'd fallen hard not only for Faith but also for the people who welcomed him, then left him alone. No flash, no pretense and no worries about cameras or who was there with whom. He liked it.

It was close to 2:00 a.m. when they waved goodbye to Marie as they left the Hole in the Wall and got into the car.

"Did you have fun?" Faith asked, her voice husky from the singing and yelling over the music.

"That was the most fun I've had in my entire life."

She chuckled and pushed his shoulder. "I don't believe you. You party with superstars every weekend."

"None of whom will take whiskey shots in between servings of lemon-pepper wings."

"They were salt-and-vinegar wings," she said with a silly smile.

"Really?"

"Yep, Marie had lemon pepper. I had salt and vinegar."

"And I ate out of every basket on the table. My nutritionist would have a heart attack."

"Eating wings like those every night will give you a heart attack," she said.

"Is that the nurse in you coming out?" He slid across the seat and leaned over her, pinning her with his arms. "Are you worried about my health now?"

Her eyes turned dreamy, and she wrapped her arms around his waist. "Maybe just a little. I don't want you to have a heart attack. I'd like to keep you around for a while."

"Oh, really? Because I'd like to stay around for a while." Her grin made his heart rate speed up. He stopped smiling to stare into her beautiful face. "I mean it, Faith. I want this to last."

"I feel like I'm in a fairy tale."

"They always have happy endings," he said.

"But they aren't real." The smile left her face. He saw the doubts starting to creep back into her eyes.

He leaned down and kissed her, pressing his body against hers until she gasped and moaned against his lips. "Does this feel real?" he asked.

"Yes." She grabbed his head and pulled it back down, and he proceeded to show her just how real this thing was between them.

Chapter 16

Faith's stomach growled as she waited for her candy bar to fall in the vending machine in the hospital's break room. She crossed her fingers and hoped the decrepit machine actually worked this time. Only to immediately curse and kick the thing when the bar got stuck.

Great. Now she was tired, frustrated, horny and hungry. She shook the machine as much as she could, but knew it was useless. A call to the security desk would get someone up here to unlock it and hand over the candy bar, but at the moment she wanted to hit something.

Twelve weeks. Three months. Ninety days. Not long in the structure of a lifetime, but it might as well have been the length of the Cretaceous period. No matter how she thought of it, seeing Irvin only sporadically during that time was torture.

Whom did she see often? The paparazzi. Every time

she thought they'd move on, she'd find out about another attempt to get information about her. Usually from "friends" she hadn't talked with since kindergarten. Or she'd leave the grocery store and someone would snap a picture.

She'd known dating Irvin would change her life, but she hadn't realized how much. Or how hard it would be to keep hoping they could make things work. She missed Irvin, but being his girlfriend was wearing her nerves down to frazzled bits.

"Faith, do you have a second?"

Faith turned away from the dangling candy bar and looked to the hospital's chief nursing officer. Lisa Williams had been nothing but nice and supportive of Faith since she'd returned, even when she'd told her it would be next to impossible for her to get a higher-ranking nursing job at the hospital despite her qualifications.

"Sure, Lisa. Let me call down to the security desk for someone to grab my candy bar and I'll come to your office."

Lisa glanced at her watch. "Come on and we'll ask Marie to call down for you."

"Sure."

She followed Lisa out of the break room. They stopped at the nurses' station, where Faith asked her friend to call about the candy bar. Marie shot a curious look between Faith and Lisa, which Faith returned with a "beats me" look of her own. Lisa made her rounds through the hospital and knew all of the nurses, but mostly it was the floor and shift managers who dealt directly with Faith and Marie. Faith was doing either really well or really badly for Lisa to come down and get her.

Or neither one, she reminded herself. In the three months since she'd returned home, random people around town had asked about her time in New York. How did it feel to be Irvin Freeman's girlfriend? What was it like to kiss him? She braced herself for Lisa's questions.

The constant presence of the paparazzi made denying her relationship with Irvin impossible. But she'd downplayed the extent of their relationship. In hindsight, that had been a good idea. They'd talked, texted and emailed a lot when he'd first left for Canada. He'd surprised her with a visit one weekend, and another time she'd driven to Atlanta to see him, but they'd had only a day before he had to get back to the set. As he got busier, the correspondence dwindled. Now she got a few sporadic texts and hadn't talked to him in over a week. If he hadn't arranged for her to come up to Canada for the weekend, she would have sworn she was one phone call away from a breakup.

"So what can I do for you?" Faith asked Lisa once they were settled in her office.

"I've wanted to talk to you since you got back from New York, but things have been hectic and I haven't had the chance."

As Faith suspected, a Q and A session on her and Irvin.

"Oh, really," she said.

"Yes. When you moved here two years ago, I hated that there wasn't a position I could offer you other than floor nurse. With your qualifications and background, you really should be sitting here instead of down on the third floor."

Faith was usually good at maintaining a poker face, but Lisa's comment surprised her so much, she was sure her face had a weird look going on.

"Umm…thanks." She wasn't quite certain of the proper response when the boss said you should have her position. She cleared her throat and schooled her features. "I was happy to get any work that would help me take care of my parents."

"Many people say things like that and don't mean them. I waited for you to complain, or be resentful for having to start at the bottom of the chain, but it never happened."

Faith shrugged. "No use in complaining about things I can't change. My parents needed me."

"Still, I want you to know that I've paid attention." Lisa shifted through the papers on her desk, picking up one. "I suppose you know that Gwendolyn put in her resignation earlier this week."

Faith frowned and slid forward in her seat. Gwendolyn was the nurse manager for the intensive-care unit. She'd been at the hospital for over twenty years and said the only things she loved more than working there were her grandchildren.

"No, I wasn't aware of that."

"Well, she did. Her daughter got a job in Colorado, and she and her husband are moving. Which means Gwendolyn's grandkids are going. She can't stand the idea of them being across the country and her daughter having to rely on strangers to look after the kids. So she's moving with them."

"Wow, that's good for her."

Lisa looked up from the paper and smiled at Faith. "And good for you, too. I want you to take her position. I know it's nothing as big as what you used to do, but it's the best I can do right now. You'll be only on the day shift, so no more overnighters, and of course I'll start you at the higher end of the pay scale considering your background."

Faith's head spun with the news. After two years of

struggling, her work was paying off. It wouldn't be close to her salary in Houston, but it was more than what she was earning now. It would allow some cushion in the family budget. No more scratching up what she could after physical therapy for her mama, doctor appointments for her dad and rehab for Love. Some of the home repairs she'd put off could be taken care of. And she'd even be able to fulfill her promise to her mama to go out more without feeling guilty.

Though she wouldn't be going out with the person she wanted.

"Are you sure?" she asked.

"I don't have a second thought. I'd also like you to represent the nurses at the hospital board meetings. I've done it for the past few years and tried to get Gwendolyn interested, but she didn't want to. It has to be a member of the managing staff. The person brings the perspective of the nursing staff to the board and hospital president. It'll be a good way to get your name in front of the higher-ups. After all, I'm planning to retire in a few years myself."

Faith bit the inside of her cheek to keep her jaw from dropping. This was unbelievable. "Of course. I'd be happy to help."

"Great." Lisa went into the details of transitioning her to the new position.

Several minutes later, Faith made her way back downstairs. Marie was reviewing a chart behind the nurses' station when Faith walked up.

"Your candy bar," Marie said, picking up the candy and waving it in Faith's direction.

"Thank you." She walked over as if in a dream and took the candy. "You won't believe what Lisa wanted."

"What, to ask you about New York?"

"I thought that was it, but no. Gwendolyn's leaving, and she's giving me her job."

Marie's brown eyes widened, and a huge grin split her face. "That's awesome, Faith!"

Faith hesitated. Marie had worked at the hospital longer than her and had complained to her about the way the hospital often moved who they wanted into certain positions instead of advertising them. That was exactly what was happening with Faith.

"Are you sure you're okay with this? It's another move they've made without posting the position."

"And finally they made a good choice. No one deserves this more than you. We've got to celebrate." Marie reached over and gave Faith a hug.

When Marie jumped up and down, Faith joined in. It was exactly what she'd wanted when she first moved home. Finally, things were looking up for her family.

Faith called her parents to tell them the great news and Marie went home with her to celebrate. When they got there, Virginia had a cake on the dining room table, and Jimmy held a bouquet of flowers.

"Where did all this come from?" Faith asked, eyeing the cake decorated with yellow flowers and Congratulations Faith in icing.

"We got it from the grocery store. You can't celebrate without cake," her dad said. He handed her the bouquet of roses and gave her a hug.

The smell of the roses instantly brought back memories of being in the flower shop with Irvin. She'd sent him a quick email about the promotion but hadn't heard back. The silence broke her heart. It was silly, she'd tried telling herself. People didn't really fall in love over a weekend. But her heartache felt pretty damn real.

"You didn't have to drive to the store," Faith said after she left her dad's embrace.

"Your dad can drive short distances," her mama said with a teasing glint in her eyes. "And you know something cool? Grocery stores have these smooth floors that allow me to move my chair around easily."

"You think you're funny," Faith said, putting the roses on the table to avoid their bittersweet fragrance. "You know what I mean. Daddy shouldn't be driving."

"Faith, dear, that weekend you went away did all of us some good," Virginia said. "You got a chance to realize that you're still young enough to have a little fun. And your dad and I realize that we've been too dependent on you since you came back."

"No, you haven't," Faith said.

Her mama rolled over and took Faith's hand in hers. "Yes, we have. We talked about it, and maybe it was the combined shock of my stroke and what Love did, but instead of learning to live with our circumstances, we let you take care of everything."

Her daddy took her other hand. "It's true, Faith. I managed to get around before your mom's stroke. It's time for you to stop spending so much of your time taking care of us and spend time taking care of yourself."

"This promotion will allow me to do both," Faith said.

Her parents both shook their heads. "But you promised me that you'd start going out, having fun and living again," Virginia said. "And now that you've got a promotion, I'm holding you to it. If you keep working yourself into the ground, we'll be forced to boot you out of the house until you start enjoying yourself again."

Marie wrapped her arm around Faith's shoulders. "Don't worry, Mr. and Mrs. Logan. I'll make sure she has fun. Besides, she's got a famous boyfriend now who'll plan more romantic vacations like the one she has coming up."

"That's right," Virginia said. "I really like Irvin. When is he gonna finish making that movie?"

Just like Faith, her parents had fallen hard for Irvin's charm in the short time they'd known him. Her mama even squealed a little bit when he referred to Faith as his girlfriend. Their only complaint about her new relationship was the media attention it drew. Jimmy had threatened to shoot one cameraman lurking in their front yard. A story that the entertainment news programs had loved.

"In a few weeks, I think," Faith said. "Hey, let's turn on some music. This is a celebration, right?"

She went to the television to turn it to one of the music stations. When she flipped it on, an entertainment show with a picture of Irvin filled the screen. Her body froze, and the air in her lungs seemed to dissipate. His hands on her body, the way he said fate brought them together, the way his eyes lit up with laughter, and the secrets they'd shared in bed—all of those memories flew across her mind. They crammed out everything except how much she missed him.

"Turn it up," Marie said. She hurried over and snatched the remote from Faith's hand.

"And things are definitely heating up on the set of the newest Irvin Freeman film," the reporter said. "Sources say that Irvin and his sexy costar Selena Jones are once again lighting things up on and off camera. The two reportedly had dinner together last night and are frequently spotted away from the set, including the overlook of Niagara Falls." As the voice-over continued, grainy photos flashed on the screen of Irvin and Selena sitting close and looking at the view, laughing on set and holding each other during what must be a love scene. "His quick romance with small-town nurse Faith Logan must be over," said the news reporter. "Because the Irvin-and-Selena chemistry is definitely sizzling."

Faith took the remote away from Marie and quickly changed the channel. Big-band music filled the silence. She didn't look away from the television screen but sensed their gazes on her.

"Faith, don't listen to that," Marie said, placing her hand on Faith's shoulder. "He wouldn't invite you up if that were true."

She shook off Marie's hand and tried for a smile. Hard to do when her throat wanted to close up from the pain. "That's what I keep telling myself."

Their relationship would always be like this. Rumors of him with other women when they were apart. How long before temptation on the road overruled feelings for a long-distance relationship? For her ex it had taken only a few weeks. She'd cared for her ex, a lot, but she hadn't fallen head over heels for him the way she had with Irvin. Now her insides burned and twisted as if wrapped in red-hot barbed wire. The pain ripped and tore at the optimism she'd had after New York.

The doorbell rang. Thank goodness for a distraction.

"I'll get that." She left their frozen silence, knowing they'd break out into hushed *poor Faith* whispers the second she walked away.

She wiped her eyes and took a deep breath when she got to the door. Whoever it was didn't deserve to have a crying fool answer. She twisted the knob and opened it.

The pain inside her froze over, then hardened into a ball of anger so fierce she literally saw red.

"What are you doing here?"

Love hiked up the duffel bag on her shoulder. The

face identical to Faith's was cool and impartial as it stared back. "I'm done with rehab. Mama said when I was done I could come home."

Chapter 17

Faith hated leaving her parents with Love out of rehab, but as Marie said, she could stay home and fight with her sister or go away for a romantic weekend with her sexy boyfriend. With the rumors of Irvin and Selena, Faith chose the weekend. Plus, she couldn't stomach seeing her parents gush over Love "graduating" from rehab and welcoming her home with open arms. As if she hadn't left them penniless. Good thing all family accounts were now controlled by Faith. Otherwise, Faith would definitely have given up this trip to see Irvin.

Kitty walked next to Faith as they entered the mock apartment where Irvin and Selena were shooting a scene from the movie. "They should be finishing up. It's just a standard love scene. I believe this is their tenth take. They've probably got it down by now."

"Tenth?" Faith asked.

Kitty shrugged. "I stopped counting at six or seven."

Faith tried to push back her wariness. He was an actor. This was his job. It didn't mean anything. But ten takes?

Kitty squeezed Faith's arms. "Don't believe the reports. There's nothing going on there. They're both in relationships now, so the chemistry is off. That's why there have been so many takes."

Straightening her shoulders, Faith nodded. Kitty gave her another squeeze then turned away. Faith appreciated Kitty's efforts to make her feel better, and she mustered up a spark of excitement about seeing Irvin work. That spark fizzled and died like wet fireworks as she watched Irvin wrap Selena in an embrace. Irvin wore a towel and Selena nothing but a lacy bra and panties.

Not real. Not real, she repeated over and over. There were cameras, lights, dozens of people watching, but it didn't stop the volatile concoction of anger and jealousy from forming a knot in her chest.

They repeated lines. The director called out instructions. The scene progressed from an embrace to lovemaking—fake lovemaking, but the thought of it still left an inerasable picture in her mind.

Finally, after Faith was sure she'd ground her teeth down to nubs, the director yelled, "Cut!" Irvin immediately turned to her, his broad, handsome smile splitting his face. Faith forced a smile of her own and waved.

He took a bottle of water one of the people on set handed him and crossed the room to her.

"You made it," he said.

"Just in time."

Irvin lowered his head to kiss her, and she averted her face. His lips brushed her cheeks.

"You've still got some of Selena's lipstick on your face." She pointed toward his lips.

Irvin wiped away the red smears. "Sorry, cutie. We can wait until I get cleaned up."

"No problem." Her voice was light and breezy. But inside a storm raged.

Not real. Not real. To make this work, she'd have to deal with this. And the paparazzi. Her stomach twisted.

"Do you have to film anything else tonight?"

"No, I'm done and can get away for the weekend." He slid his arm around her waist and pulled her against him.

The feel of his solid chest and the hypnotic cadence of his accent eased away some of her discomfort. Faith wrapped her arms around his neck.

"Where are we going?"

"It's going to be just the two of us this weekend. No Kitty, no entourage, no intrusions. How does that sound?"

"Absolutely wonderful."

"Good. Now give me a second to wrap up some things here and we'll continue with our plans." He rubbed his nose against hers then let her go and strolled over to the director.

The entire crew seemed to gravitate toward him. Even the director seemed to soak in Irvin's words as they discussed the scene they'd just shot. He seemed so right for this world. She wasn't sure if she ever would feel as comfortable in her own skin as he looked on set.

Selena walked over. She'd put on a white bathrobe over the underwear Irvin had torn off based on the director's instructions and twisted her long raven locks into a knot on the top of her head.

"Faith, I'm so glad you came. Irvin has driven everyone crazy with missing you." Selena leaned in and wrapped Faith in a big hug. "You guys have a great weekend, okay?"

When Selena pulled back, Faith nodded. "Umm… sure. Thanks, Selena."

Selena hesitated. "I know today was kind of rough on you. My fiancé was the same way when we first started dating. Remember, it's *just* acting." She pointed to the set. "What he says, does and feels about you is real."

The tightness in Faith's shoulders diminished. "I'm trying to remember that."

"It'll get easier with time. And I think you'll be around for a while. Seriously, all he does is talk about you."

Faith chuckled, and she felt herself giving the other woman a genuine smile. "Thank you, Selena."

Selena walked away, and Faith glanced across the room and caught Irvin's eye. His face lit up, and his grin warmed every inch of her body. Her breath escaped in a soft sigh. She loved him. Realistically they'd only end in heartbreak, but for now she'd hold on to her love and the way he looked at her. And maybe, just maybe, if they did end, the memories would get her through the pain.

Irvin squeezed Faith's hand as they walked in and out of shops along Queen Street in the small town of Niagara-on-the-Lake. Sweat trickled down his back, not from the bright sun filtering through the tree-lined street but from nerves. He hadn't figured out the best way to ask Faith and her family to move to New York.

He was falling in love with her. He had realized that one morning when he'd spoken to her after she'd finished a night shift at the hospital. The sound of her voice had instantly brightened his mood after a long day on set. Three months in and he was absolutely smitten. He wanted her to be waiting at his place whenever he finished a job. Not thousands of miles away.

He glanced over at Faith, who looked fantastic in

a bright green dress that brushed the tops of her feet. Green-and-gold flats and a thin gold bracelet were her only adornments. Not that she needed more.

New York would be good for her career and her family. More choices in doctors for her parents' care. Better options in the nursing field. Plus, they'd be together. He swallowed hard. If only he could convince her moving wasn't completely crazy.

"Are you having a good time?" he asked.

Her grin warmed him better than the sun. "I am. This town is beautiful."

"It's considered one of the most stunning small towns in Canada. I thought you would prefer coming here over the hustle and bustle of a larger city."

She slipped her arm through his and leaned into his side. "Look at you, learning my tastes."

"Isn't that what I'm supposed to do? Know what my lady likes and get it for her?"

"I think you're trying to spoil me."

"If you consider this little getaway an attempt at spoiling you, then, yes, I am."

She chuckled and pulled him closer. Irvin took solace in the small movement. The look in her eye after shooting his scenes with Selena told him Faith would have a hard time watching him work. He could only imagine the thoughts that went through her head. He'd made a point to reassure her rumors of him and Selena were false.

Maybe admitting the depth of his feelings would ease her fears further and make his offer for her and her family to move to New York more appealing.

Faith sighed and leaned her head against his shoulder. "If only every weekend could be like this."

Just the motivation he needed. "Every weekend could."

She shook her head. "I didn't tell you because I didn't want to spoil the weekend."

"Tell me what?" He led her to one of the wooden benches on the side of the street and sat.

"Love came home right before I left. She's done with rehab, apparently, and Mama said she could stay."

He took her hands in his. "Are you okay?"

"For the most part. I started to stay, but again, my parents practically pushed me out the door." She grinned and shrugged. "She no longer has access to their accounts. Everything is in my name, and all information is locked away with Marie. I needed to leave or else I would have said something I'd later regret. This is a terrible time for her to return. I just got promoted. Now there's another mouth to feed."

"You were promoted?"

Her tight frown turned into a smile. "Yes, to floor nurse. Didn't you get my email yesterday?"

"Sorry, it was a long day. I haven't checked any email."

Disappointment shadowed her eyes. "Oh."

He squeezed her hands. "That's fantastic, Faith." But he knew a promotion would be less incentive for her to move to New York.

"I should be happy, not freaking out because my twin is back."

"Faith, you aren't responsible for your sister's actions, and you can't walk around waiting for her to fail again. Be cautious. But if your parents were able to move on and forgive, maybe you should, too."

"How can I forgive what she did?"

"Because she was in a very dark place. People in dark places do terrible things. Keep your guard up, but if she really finished the program, support her while she's clean."

188 A New York Kind of Love

"And if she slips up?"

The worry in her eyes made him wish he could guarantee Love would never screw up again. But he knew that was out of both of their hands. He brushed his hand across her soft cheek. "Send her back to rehab, or get her out of the house if she refuses help."

Her brows drew together. "I don't like those options."

Irvin swallowed and scooted closer. Now was the time. "There is another option."

"What?"

"Move you and your parents to New York."

Faith laughed. "Yeah, right."

He tugged on her arm until she looked at him. He didn't smile. "I'm serious. You can come stay with me. I—"

"My parents wouldn't even consider moving. And I can't leave them alone with my sister."

"I talked with your mum. She wants you to be happy."

Faith snatched her hand away. "You asked my mama already?"

"I wanted her to know that I'm serious about us. And to give you a reason to ignore any ridiculous rumors about me and Selena or anyone else."

"How about not shooting a love scene with her ten times?"

"Those ten takes were because it's hard to fake desire for Selena when all I can think about is you."

She sputtered, her mouth opening and closing as she struggled to speak.

He kept going. "You know I'm not sleeping with Selena, so why don't you tell me what's so terrible about me wanting you to move to New York?"

"Nothing, but you can't go behind my back and make

plans without asking me. You can't run my life the way Kitty runs yours."

Her words hit so close to the truth, he fell silent. Then his mobile rang, preventing him from replying. Faith crossed her arms and looked away. He pulled the device from his pocket.

One glance at the screen and his jaw dropped. "It's Kevin Lipinski," Irvin said, surprised.

Faith's frown transformed into an eager smile. She motioned toward the phone. "Answer it."

He quickly accepted and brought the phone to his ear. "Irvin, this is Kevin Lipinski. Did I catch you at a bad time?" Kevin asked in a brisk, no-nonsense tone.

Irvin glanced at Faith's curious expression. "I've got a minute."

"Good, good. Listen, I got around to reading your screenplay last night, and I've got to say, I'm impressed."

Irvin slid forward on the bench, excitement pounding through his veins. "Oh, really." His ability to sound so casual should've earned him an instant Oscar.

"Yes, the story of the son observing his mother in denial of her husband's alcohol problem. The way the kid tried to protect her, but ultimately couldn't save either of them. It really touched something in me. Where did you dream this story up?"

"I didn't. It's my story," he said.

"I should have known. That much emotion and realism couldn't be made up. Look, I know you're in the middle of filming, but why don't you fly out to San Francisco so we can talk. You had mentioned wanting to direct."

"I do."

"I'll consider it."

Irvin found Kevin's not-flat-out-refusal encouraging. "Look, Kevin, I'm wrapping up the majority of my scenes this week. I can fly out to see you after that."

"Sounds good. Just call me when you're in town and we'll do lunch. I'm looking forward to working with you."

"Same here." He ended the call, then let out a joyous shriek. He turned to Faith. "He loved my script and wants to talk about making it into a movie. I'm going to San Francisco next week to discuss it."

"That's fantastic." She wrapped her arms around his neck. "I'm so happy for you."

He pulled back. "It sure took him long enough."

"Good things come to those who wait."

He met her eye. "I don't want to wait on us. Faith, please consider—"

She placed her hand gently over his mouth. "Let's talk about that later. You've just got great news. Let's celebrate." She leaned in and kissed him.

Her kiss combined with the euphoria pulsing in his veins to awaken his arousal instantly.

A voice broke the moment. "Excuse me. Are you Irvin Freeman?"

Irvin turned to a woman holding up a camera phone.

"I am," he said, trying to sound pleasant. Trying to remember fans paid for his lifestyle. But he could think only of his moment with Faith being broken and their previous unresolved conversation.

"Oh my God, I love your movies!" the woman squealed. "Can I get a picture?"

Irvin glanced at Faith, who nodded. Then he looked back at the woman. "Sure—one picture."

One picture turned into two, and two pictures led to a crowd forming. Thirty minutes later he and Faith were finally able to escape. They made their way to a bed-

and-breakfast located at one of the town's wineries. He'd reserved every room so that he and Faith could be alone.

"Faith, we need to talk about what I asked," he said once they were in their room.

Faith shook her head. "Not right now." She pushed the sleeves of her dress down her shoulders. She did a little shake, and the material softly slid to her feet. Irvin's mouth went dry at the sight of her in the skimpy bra and panties. "Now we're celebrating."

She strolled over to him and pulled him down for a kiss. Irvin lost himself in her embrace, but also felt another hurdle grow between him and Faith.

Chapter 18

Faith refused to let Irvin talk to her about moving to New York any further. For the rest of the weekend, whenever he brought up the subject, she found a way to change it. Or someone conveniently interrupted them to get an autograph or picture. Even during the short car ride back to Niagara Falls, she'd distracted him with questions about his life in London. She didn't want to move, and based on his phone call from Kevin Lipinski, he was about to get a lot busier. Meaning their relationship would become even harder to maintain.

"This was one of the best weekends of my life," Faith said as they entered the hotel where the cast and crew were staying during the movie shoot. "I'll never forget it."

"There will be plenty more weekends like this," Irvin said.

Faith smiled and nodded. "Sure."

She broke eye contact to stare across the lobby. There

wouldn't be more weekends like this. She would end things once she got back to South Carolina. This wasn't the life for her, not with the constant rumors and intrusive fans. Telling him they should move on would be hard, but her one consolation was that she'd get to keep her feelings under wraps. He'd never know she'd fallen deeply in love.

"Are you okay?" Irvin moved into her line of vision, concern etched on his handsome face.

"I'm great." She forced cheer into her tone that sounded almost legitimate.

He frowned and questioned her with his eyes.

Faith's cell phone rang. She quickly diverted her full attention to the device.

Kitty hurried over. "Irvin, you got a sec?"

Faith's parents' number flashed on her screen. "Go talk to Kitty while I take this." She walked away and answered the call before he could respond.

"Are you going to be back tomorrow?" Love's voice snapped through the phone.

Faith tensed, bracing herself for bad news. "Yes, first thing. Why?"

"Because I just chased away another cameraman who tried to snap pictures of Mama and Daddy in the backyard."

Faith put a hand on her hip and scowled. "What?"

"You heard me. Ever since you were spotted on your romantic weekend with that movie star, this guy has been showing up trying to snap pictures." Love's voice dripped with annoyance. "This is all your fault."

"Hold up. I know you're not trying to chastise me."

"Look, Faith, I'll admit from now until the end of time that I screwed up. Stealing from Mama and Daddy was my rock bottom. I finished rehab and I'm staying clean. In a few weeks I'm moving to Greenville with a woman I met in rehab. We got jobs and are starting over away from the people and places that have always led us to trouble."

Faith's mouth fell open. She quickly snapped it shut. "You're what?"

"Moving. Getting a job. Sending money back to Mama and Daddy to pay for my mistakes." Love sighed. "Look, I don't expect you to believe me or believe in me, but I'm trying, all right? It'll take a while, but I'm going to do better."

Confidence and resolve strengthened Love's voice. Faith hadn't heard that type of power in her sister's tone since they were little girls. And she had missed it.

"I believe you."

Several seconds passed before Love responded. "Thank you. But you've got to do something about the paparazzi. Mama and Daddy aren't going to say anything, but it's bothering them, too."

"It'll all be ending soon," Faith said.

Irvin walked over and placed a hand on her lower back. He mouthed the words *Everything okay?* and she nodded.

"Hey, I've got to go. Tell them not to worry. I'll take care of it." She ended the call and slipped the phone into her purse.

"What do you have to handle?"

"Just a cameraman hanging around the house. They keep popping up since you and I started dating."

He rubbed his forehead and groaned. "I'm so sorry." He dropped his hand. "How do you want to handle it?"

By leaving you. The thought made her heart hurt. "We'll figure something out."

Irvin wrapped an arm around her shoulders, and she slid hers around his waist.

"There's something I've wanted to tell you all weekend," Irvin said as they walked to the elevator.

"What's that?"

Irvin used his finger to tilt up her chin. His deep stare held complete adoration that she'd seen only from guys looking at the woman they loved. Her body thrummed with anticipation.

"Faith, I—"

"Ready for another long week, Irvin?" One of the costars of the film, action star Lathan Taylor, walked up.

Faith's shoulders slumped, and Irvin's mouth tightened before he faced the action star and shrugged.

"The harder we work, the better the end product," Irvin said.

Lathan stepped onto the elevator with Faith and Irvin and kept up a constant stream of conversation about the filming. Faith normally would have been excited to meet Lathan, but she could muster up only tight smiles and stiff nods whenever he cracked a joke.

Maybe it was wishful thinking, or she really didn't want to break things off with Irvin, but she'd hoped Irvin would say he loved her. Not that his confession would change their situation much. She still couldn't move to New York and be left behind whenever he traveled to whatever city in the world his next movie would be filmed in.

They all got off on the top floor, where most of the cast were staying, and parted ways with the actor.

"Now you can tell everyone you met Lathan Taylor," Irvin said. "I'm surprised you weren't more excited. You're always excited to meet celebrities…that aren't me."

She chuckled. "You're never going to let that go, are you?"

He pulled the key card for the room out of his back pocket and slid it into the door. "Not anytime soon."

Irvin opened the door and stepped back for Faith to go in first. Faith slipped her finger into the belt loops of his navy slacks. She walked backward into the room and tugged him along.

"I'll tell you now, it was very difficult to suppress my fangirl sigh when I first laid eyes on you."

One side of his mouth rose in a sexy half smile. "Was that before or after you decided to pretend as if you didn't want to win?"

"Before, and the second you told me to relax because you don't bite was the first time in my life I actually wanted to be bitten." She jerked on his belt loop until his body brushed hers.

Irvin's brows rose and his dark eyes lit up. Sliding one long arm around her waist, he pulled her into the seductive heat of his body. "I'd prefer to do a little nibbling." He kicked the door closed with his foot.

"*Nibbling* is such a silly word."

He lightly nipped at the side of her neck. Trembles scattered across her skin. "Does this feel silly?" His accent deepened with his desire.

Faith's eyes fluttered closed and she shook her head. His nibble was far from silly and had her ready to strip in the living area and beg for him to do exactly what he was doing to other parts of her body.

The sound of footsteps running from the bedroom made them both freeze.

"Welcome back, baby!" a woman's voice called.

Faith pushed Irvin's chest. He looked just as surprised as she did.

"Ooh, you brought company," the woman said.

Irvin looked over Faith's shoulders. His body stiffened and his eyes narrowed. Faith spun around. The superfan she'd seen twice during her trip to New York stood completely naked in the middle of the room.

Faith's eyes bulged so hard she feared she had strained the muscles.

Irvin pushed Faith behind him. "How did you get in my room? This floor is monitored."

"You said some other time." The pitch of the woman's whine was high enough to shatter glass.

Faith glared at the back of Irvin's head. "You told her what?"

He turned to Faith. "I tell lots of people that. I don't mean it."

The woman rushed over. "You meant it with me. I felt it. Just give me time. I'll show you things you've never seen before."

The woman's eyes darted from Faith to Irvin. Faith couldn't tell if she was crazy or just hyperexcited to be there.

"Faith, call security," Irvin said.

Faith edged away.

A bewildered smile covered the woman's face. "No! Irvin, I love you." She reached for Irvin.

He stepped back. "Faith, call!"

Faith hurried to the phone.

"No," the woman yelled.

Faith looked over her shoulder, and the woman barreled into Faith's side at the same time. They fell to the floor. *No, this fool didn't just knock me to the floor!*

Faith rolled over and tried to push her off without touching too much of the crazy fan's naked body. But the lady must have covered herself in baby oil or something because Faith's hands just slipped across her feverish skin.

"You're not calling security. Give me a chance."

Pain shot through Faith's scalp. *She just pulled my...* Another sharp pain. That was it. Faith used her elbows, legs, knees and fists to fight the woman off of her.

Irvin was there instantly to pull the slippery woman off. She fought them both with earnest.

"He's mine. I should have won that contest." She screamed when Irvin finally got her around the waist and pulled her off Faith. She kicked and reached for Faith again. "It would be me in this hotel if I would've won."

"Not bloody likely," Irvin grunted as another of the woman's kicks connected with his shin.

The door to the room burst open. Kitty and her entourage flooded the room. For once Faith welcomed the publicist's intrusion. In a matter of seconds Kitty had two guys grab the fan. Minutes later, security guards were dragging the woman, naked and screaming, from Irvin's room.

Faith escaped to the bedroom while security and Kitty grilled everyone to find out how the woman had got in Irvin's room. Irvin came into the bedroom and sat next to her on the king-size bed.

"Are you okay?"

She shook her head. "I was just in a wrestling match with a naked woman on the floor. No, I'm not okay."

"Faith," he sighed. "I didn't invite her here."

Faith rubbed her aching temples. Her mind replayed the last scene. Interrupted by visions of the cameramen hanging around her family, and media reports of Irvin and Selena.

"I believe you. Something is obviously wrong with her." She dropped her hands. "But I can't do this. The paparazzi, the constant interruptions, the crazy naked women in hotel rooms."

"Faith, don't." His voice hardened. "Not over this."

She jumped up from the bed and paced back and forth. "It's not just this. I'm not moving to New York."

Irvin stood and took her arm. His pleading eyes bored into hers. "Then don't. We can make this work."

"No, we can't." Her heart broke with each second that passed, and she lowered her gaze to the floor. "The past few months were like a dream come true."

His hand on her arm tightened. "Don't."

"And I'll always remember the time we spent together."

"That sounds like a bad line from a movie."

"I'm not good at breakups."

He cupped her face in his hands. "Then don't break things off."

Kitty popped her head through the doorway. "Irvin, the cops are here. They need a statement."

Irvin groaned. "They can wait."

Faith pulled out of his embrace. "There's no need. I'm leaving."

"Faith." Irvin reached for her, but she dodged his hand.

"Kitty," she said, "please move my flight up if possible."

Kitty's concerned gaze went from Irvin to Faith. "If it's what you really want."

Faith took a deep breath, still smelling the crazy woman's perfume. What if someone equally as crazy went after her parents?

"It is." She spoke the lie with a confidence she didn't feel.

"Faith, cutie, don't do this." Irvin's warm hand clasped

hers. He tried to pull her into his arms. She wanted to go into his embrace and forget everything.

"If you won't talk to the police, then I will." Faith pulled out of his reach and refused to meet his eyes. She rushed past Kitty, knowing that if she looked at Irvin, she'd never walk away.

Chapter 19

The flight attendant told Irvin they were about twenty minutes from landing, so he pulled out his mobile to make the call. He'd flown to San Francisco to meet with Kevin the day before, and the two had made plans to begin production early the following year. Kevin, straightforward as he was, wanted to start earlier, but Irvin refused. He'd worked constantly on his career even before he struck it big. He was taking a few months off. If he wanted to win Faith back, he'd have to.

Therefore, he expected this phone call not to go very well.

"Irvin, where are you?" Kitty wasted no time waiting for his reply. She took off like a race car on a speedway. "Since you're finished wrapping up your scenes in Canada, I've got some things lined up for you. *GQ* magazine wants you to do a spread for their November issue, so we'll have to line up the photo shoot in the next week or so. Also, they're looking for several celebrity guest spots on the sitcom *Dolls and Calls*. That show is hot right now, and everyone who's anyone is guest starring. One spot calls for a sexy male chef, and you'd be perfect for it. Auditions start tomorrow, but once you let them know you're interested, you'll be a shoo-in."

Irvin rubbed his temple as Kitty rattled on. Of course it wouldn't cross her mind that he might want to relax after twelve weeks of filming. Then again, he'd never rested before, so she was only doing her job.

"Kitty, I just left San Francisco, where I had a meeting with Kevin Lipinski. He liked my screenplay and wants me to direct. We're going to start production next year."

"That's great, Irvin," Kitty said with what he could tell was hesitant enthusiasm. "I'll be sure to work that into your latest round of promos. And word on the street is you're getting the part for that new superhero movie. Filming is set to begin in December."

"I'm not taking the part."

There was laughter on the other end of the phone. "You're funny, Irvin. Now—"

"I'm serious, Kitty. I've already turned it down. I'm going to take the rest of the year off."

"Why?"

It was Irvin's turn to laugh. Kitty always went at her job 110 percent. He didn't think she'd ever taken a vacation in the time they'd worked together. On the rare days he did rest, she was always out there promoting.

"Because I'm tired, and I want to take a break. I want to live my life for a while without the constant flash of cameras. If this works out with Kevin, then I'm going to go for other directing jobs. I'm ready to get behind the camera."

"Where are you now?" Kitty asked, her suspicion as clear as the sky he glimpsed out the aircraft window.

"On a plane."

"Where are you going?"

"I'm not telling you, because I don't want you sending word ahead that'll have dozens of paparazzi waiting." Dante had a private airstrip at his home in San Francisco, so Irvin had taken his friend's jet to avoid the cameras.

"I can guess," Kitty said. "You're going to South Carolina. I knew you wouldn't give up so easily. You've finally fallen in love."

He couldn't tell by her tone if she was surprised, happy, pissed or confused. "I have, and I missed her the second she left. I think she won that contest for a reason. I was already tired and looking for an excuse to slow down. The screenplay was one reason. Faith became the other."

"Am I fired?" Kitty was direct as usual, but for the first time Irvin heard uncertainty in Kitty's voice.

"No, Kitty, you're not fired. After everything you've done for me, I wouldn't sack you so casually. I'm moving behind the camera, but I'm sure I'll still need your services occasionally. Just consider this your opportunity to put your efforts into making the next handsome guy Hollywood's biggest star."

Kitty chuckled. "I couldn't be lucky enough to come across another talent as good as yours." She sighed into the phone. "I wish you well, Irvin."

That surprised him. "Thank you, Kitty."

"You're welcome. Not everyone is lucky enough to have love strike as hard as it did with you two. Honestly, this move to directing and away from the spotlight is probably the best way to make it work. Just don't forget to invite me to the wedding. I expect to be maid of honor or best man or something. It was my idea to do the contest," she said. He could hear the smile in her voice.

"When we get there, I promise not to forget."

They ended the call, and he settled back into the soft leather seat. When they got there. He'd never thought about getting married before. Amazing what a difference a few days could make.

Irvin landed at the same private airport he and Faith had flown into. He'd already arranged to have a car waiting for him there. As soon as he got out and breathed deeply of the fresh air, he knew he'd made the right decision. He'd spent only a day and a half with Faith in her hometown, but that time felt more like home than years living in New York.

"You've given my airstrip more action than it's seen in years," Gary said. He stood next to the car waiting for Irvin.

"I hope to give it more attention."

"That'll be good news to whoever buys it from me."

Irvin took a look at the strip and the surrounding landscape. Thick pine trees and none of the noise that had been the constant backdrop of his life. "Do you own the land around it?"

"Most of it."

"Maybe I'll buy it from you," Irvin said.

Gary's eyebrows rose. "Now, why would you do that?"

"I'm thinking about moving here. If Faith will have me."

"Hmm…after the television report about that crazy fan sneaking into your room, and Faith telling the few cameramen hanging around town that you two were done, most folks around here didn't think you'd be coming back."

"That's what they get for thinking," Irvin said, throwing back the line Gary had tossed out when he and Faith first flew into the strip.

Gary laughed and stuck out his hand. "If you're serious, then we can talk. I've got no reason to keep the strip, and I'd rather sell it to you and Faith than someone else. She deserves a lot of happiness."

Irvin took Gary's hand and shook it. "I plan to give her a lot of happiness."

He said his goodbyes to Gary and got in the car for the short ride to Faith's parents' house, thinking about the airstrip. Once again, fate had stepped in and shown him he was on the right track. There was enough acreage out there to build a house and properly secure it. He could update the airstrip and fly directly in and out with no problems, making it even easier for him or Faith to travel. By the time the driver pulled up to Faith's home, Irvin's mind was bounding with excitement.

The car pulled into the driveway, and he got out without waiting for the driver to open the door. His hands were full of the gifts he hoped would remind her why they belonged together. He could see Faith in the backyard hanging sheets on the clothesline. Music playing from somewhere in back must have prevented her from hearing the car, because she didn't turn around. He preferred to surprise her anyway.

He went through the gate in the picket fence surrounding the house and crept up to her. She bent over to pick up another sheet, humming to herself and completely oblivious to him. As she reached up to hang the sheet, he took her arm in his.

"Guess who," he said, spinning her around and kissing her.

Something wasn't right. He sensed it a second before she jerked back and kneed him in the balls. He doubled over as pain exploded through his groin. His gifts hit the ground.

"Who the hell are you?" he asked through gritted teeth.

He glanced up through watery eyes into a face that was similar to Faith's, but wasn't hers.

"I'd ask the same thing, but I've figured that out," the evil body double said.

"Love?" he said, slowly standing straight though the pain had barely subsided.

Love twirled her hand and bowed. "The one and only."

Thank God for that, he thought. "I thought you moved to Greenville."

"I did. Just here for the weekend." She propped a hand on her hip and cocked her head to the side. "I thought Faith broke up with you."

"She did. I'm here to win her back."

Footsteps came closer from the rear. "You are?"

He spun toward Faith, then grimaced at the aftershock of discomfort caused by the sudden move. "I am."

She was in the outfit he'd first seen her in back in New York—the lavender tank top and cutoff jean shorts that had driven him mad from the start. He'd known he'd missed her, but not until that second did he realize how *much* he'd missed her.

He took a step toward her, which was more of a limp. Concern knitted her brow, and she hurried forward. "I saw what happened. Sorry about that."

"So am I." He flung a glare over his shoulder at her twin.

"My bad," Love said. "I'm not good with strange men grabbing me suddenly."

"I see that," he said. He looked to Faith standing next to him. "Is there somewhere we can talk?"

"Come in the house."

"I'll finish up out here and give you two some privacy," Love said.

"Yes," Irvin said, his voice barely hiding his eagerness to get away. "Do that."

The twins shared a look. He had a sneaking feeling that they could communicate an entire conversation that way.

He picked up a bouquet of roses and a black folder. He gave the flowers to Faith. "They're from Belles Fleurs," he said. Faith's eyes widened before her lips curved in a sweet smile. "I wrote the card myself. Xavier and Diane thought it was very romantic." He took a step forward and winced at the residual pain.

Faith blinked and broke eye contact. She waved him toward the house. "Come on. Let's get you some ice," she said.

Faith's entire body shook from the shock of having Irvin show up. She'd assumed he'd accept things were over and move on. She hadn't prepared herself for him popping up.

She sat him at the kitchen table. "Let me get the ice."

He sat, then twisted on the seat as if trying to get comfortable. "No, it's starting to get better."

"Love's the more aggressive twin."

He grunted. "I noticed. Are you okay with her being here?"

She sat in the chair next to him and placed the flowers on the table. Their fragrance immediately transported her back to their night in New York. "I'm taking it one day at a time. She wants to prove she's better, so I decided to keep an open mind."

When they made eye contact, the electric heat the man created with just a look jolted her system. His eyes burned with desire, making it hard for her to breathe.

Faith jerked her eyes away and ran her hands across the tablecloth. She wanted to grin, laugh, jump with excitement that he was there, but the circumstances hadn't changed. "I need to stay here to support her and my parents during this process. We all need to heal."

Irvin put his hand on hers. "Then we'll help her."

"We?"

"Yes, we."

She shook her head. "This is my family's problem. You don't have to do anything. You can't do anything. You're in New York or going to California."

She tried to pull her hand away, but he held firm.

"Who's going to support you through all this? Faith, you deserve so much, and all I want to do is give you everything you deserve."

The look in his eye was so sincere, and the confidence in his voice made her want to accept his offer.

"I appreciate that, but nothing's changed, Irvin. It would have been better if you hadn't come." She stood and went over to the refrigerator. "Do you want some lemonade? My mama made it fresh this morning. She and Daddy went to the grocery store to pick up a few things."

He held the black folder in front of her. She slowly closed the fridge, and with shaky hands, she opened the folder to reveal a charcoal portrait of her and Irvin, signed by Carl.

"Carl says he can't wait to see you again," Irvin said. "He moved into the apartment and started AA. It took some time, but he's healing. I think the same can happen with Love."

Faith smiled. "I'm happy to hear that." She wanted Carl to overcome his demons, just like she wanted Love to overcome hers. Hope for them both filled her. As she stared at the picture, her hope for them blossomed into hope for Irvin and herself.

"I didn't come here to just bribe you with gifts." Irvin turned her to face him. He took a deep breath and stared into her eyes. "I came here to tell you that I love you."

It took a second for what he said to wiggle through her mind. She blinked several times, trying to make sense of words she'd only imagined hearing.

"You love me?"

"Yes. I knew it was happening for a long time, but it wasn't until you left Canada that it really hit me. I would have told you then, but we were always interrupted."

"That's part of the problem. Someone is always going to interrupt us. Most women would jump at the chance to be your girlfriend. For the apartment in New York and the offer to have their parents moved. But I can't live that life. I can't do the constant cameras, fight the crowds everywhere I go or have Kitty organize every move I make. My life is here. My parents are here—"

"What if I told you that I'm taking the rest of the year off, and that I called Kitty on my way here to let her know while I appreciate everything she's done for me, she's free to find another upcoming actor to make a star?"

"The rest of the year off? Irvin, you'll go crazy."

"No, the old Irvin would go crazy. The one who came to New York in order to reinvent himself and forget what he left behind. I don't have to hustle anymore. My fortune is built, my career bigger than I ever expected." He wasn't bragging. She knew that. In fact, he gave a self-effacing shrug. Then a huge grin lit up his face. "I struck a deal with Kevin to back my screenplay. I'll be directing, Faith. But I made the deal with the caveat that we won't begin work until after the New Year."

"You did all of that?"

"All of that. Faith, I was growing tired of the hustle before I met you. I checked my email constantly, waiting for Kevin to call and give me an excuse to take a step back. Then I met you, and like so many of the heroes I played, I fell for the girl in a weekend. I love you, but I know what fame can do to a relationship. I don't want my stardom to ruin us before we get started. We'll take the next year to get this thing right. Right for us, your parents, even your knee-happy twin."

She tried to think of something to say. It should definitely be cute, or funny, or profound, but the only thing she could think of was how much she loved him and how she couldn't imagine he actually was willing to take a chance on loving her.

"Why? Why would you do this?"

"It's like I told you in New York. I believe in fate. It told me it was time to leave my family and go to New York. It made me wander into an audition for a small role in a play that in turn grabbed Kitty's attention and made her introduce me to all the right people. Fate is the reason I got the role that made me a star after I lost another role that everyone swore would make my career. And fate pulled your name out of thousands and brought you to New York. I trust that, and I'm not going to just let it go."

Her heart beat so fast, she wondered if it was going to short-circuit. Love and excitement filled her from head to toe. "I love you, too. Man, Irvin, I love you so much, but I was so afraid to say it. So afraid to trust it. Life kept throwing me curveballs, and I couldn't believe that this thing between us was actually happening."

The words rushed out of her, each one making his smile bigger and brighter. "It really happened." He lowered his head to kiss her. "And I've got several months to show you how much I love you."

Chapter 20

Irvin's leg shook so hard next to Faith that the seats vibrated. She placed her hand on his tuxedo-clad thigh and gave a gentle squeeze. He looked her way and mouthed *Sorry*. Her show of calm was just that, a show. The Dolby Theatre was packed with all of Hollywood royalty, as usual for the Academy Awards. That same royalty held their collective breath as the top awards were about to be announced.

After two years with Irvin, Faith was pretty good at containing her fangirl squeals when she met new celebrities. But tonight she'd nearly fainted when some of the legendary members of Hollywood's elite came over to wish Irvin well.

She'd been excited and petrified about the red carpet. Years of watching the fashion critiques after the awards shows had her freaking out from the moment it was announced that Irvin and his film were nominated for best director, best screenplay and best picture. Thankfully, Kitty agreed to help and ensured Faith got the most beautiful gown, an aquamarine, one-shoulder Vera Wang creation that wowed on the red carpet.

It had taken almost a year for the media to calm some of its constant attention on Irvin. Him moving to a rural county in South Carolina and building a sweeping estate around the private airfield had generated its share of buzz. And by the time that died down, word of his partnership with Kevin Lipinski caused another rush of media excitement. They'd thought it was finally mellowing out when he'd got the nomination.

They'd become extra diligent at keeping their relationship private. Both to protect their relationship and to keep her family out of the spotlight. For Faith and Irvin, there were no more scheduled appearances, constant partying or intense schedules. They'd found a balance, and thanks to having a private airfield, she was able to dart across the country to visit with Irvin when they'd begun shooting. She still couldn't believe she was living this life.

"And now the nominees for best director..." Selena said from the stage.

Unable to contain her nervousness, Faith squeezed Irvin's hand. "No matter what happens, I'm proud of you," she whispered.

She didn't hear the names of all the nominees for the blood rushing between her ears. Her palm became increasingly sweaty in his, and her heart pounded so hard, she thought it'd burst from her chest. It wasn't until he went rigid beside her, then squeezed her hand, that she snapped out of it. She saw heads turned in their direction, smiles everywhere. In what seemed like slow motion, she looked at Irvin and found him grinning.

"I won." Disbelief sounded in his voice.

"You won," she breathed.

He grabbed both sides of her face and kissed her senseless. She laughed and cried at the same time.

"You'd better get up there," she said.

He kissed her again and stood to sprint up the aisle to the stage. Faith joined in with the thunderous applause filling the theater.

Irvin hugged Selena, who kissed his cheek. Then he held out the Oscar to look at it. He slapped a hand over his forehead and turned back to the crowd. "I can't believe I'm actually up here," he said. "I've imagined this moment all of my life, but until you're actually up here... Yeah, it's brilliant. Of course, I want to thank my agent, and my publicist, Kitty Brown, who stuck with me through my voluntary exile." That drew a few laughs from the crowd. "Thanks to the cast and crew, who did such a fantastic job. You guys made directing almost easy. Thank you to Kevin Lipinski for taking a chance on an unproved director and on a screenplay that long before I approached him, I wasn't sure I would ever finish. Many of you know that Eric's story is my story, and it took a lot for me to get the words on paper." He held up the award and shook his head. "Wow, this is completely real."

Several people clapped and cheered.

"I know I'll forget people, so I won't try to remember anyone else, but I'd be remiss if I didn't thank the most important person in the world to me. Fate brought her to me for a reason. I don't have much of a family, but she became my family. And her parents have been wonderful in welcoming me into their midst. Faith..." He looked in her direction. "I love you and can't imagine celebrating this award with anyone else. The only thing that would make this better is if you marry me. So, please, say you'll be my wife."

A gasp, then applause went through the crowd. Tears blurred Faith's vision as the voices of everyone around her became a distant hum. Irvin had brought up marriage only a few times. Even though he'd built the estate, asked her and her family to live there with him and shown the world that she was the woman in his life, she hadn't expected a real proposal. They'd just found the relationship balance that worked for them.

It didn't stop her from making her choice.

"Yes!" she yelled back as the music played and Irvin was ushered off the stage. She hurried across the aisle and ran backstage. She pushed past other celebrities, makeup artists and members of the television crew to the postacceptance interview area.

Kitty and her team were prepping him for all of the usual *how do you feel?* questions. The instant he saw her through the crowd, he left the interview area and ran over to her.

"You're crazy," she said as he swept her up in his arms and swung her around.

"Then you'll be married to a crazy Oscar winner," he said.

He set her down, and they both grinned.

"I can't believe you did that," she said through her smile.

"I can't believe you haven't answered me yet."

"You didn't hear me? I screamed yes." She wrapped her arms around his neck and kissed his cheek repeatedly. "Yes, yes, yes, you wonderful, crazy man."

"I hear you now, cutie," he said, laughing. "I love you so much, Faith." Happiness, excitement and tenderness were written all over his face. "Fate selected you, and I always trust in fate."

She kissed him, and cameras flashed everywhere. For the first time, she didn't care. They could post these pictures all over the internet. It was the happiest day of her life, and she wanted everyone to see it. Finally, fate hadn't played a cruel trick on her. It had brought her the love of her life.

* * * * *

A bet worth the risk...

J.M. Jeffries

DRAWING
Hearts

Overseeing the boutiques at her grandmother's casino is a lucky break for fashion buyer Kenzie Russell. But Kenzie longs to launch her own designer line. Reed Watson, the übersexy tech guru who's fixing the casino's software glitches is a distraction. They're opposites except when it comes to their powerful attraction. But with a secret adversary trying to cause chaos, everything is at stake—including their once-in-a-lifetime connection...

PASSION'S GAMBLE

Available January 2016!

"Readers get to see the natural and believable progression of a relationship from colleagues to friends to lovers...the journey is a good one..." —*RT Book Reviews* on LOVE TAKES ALL

Love's a game
without rules

Regina Hart

KIMANI® ROMANCE

Passion
PLAY

THE ANDERSON FAMILY

Regina Hart

Passion
PLAY

With her law school reunion fast approaching, Rose Beharie needs a handsome, successful date that will prove to her ex that she's moved on. Sales executive Donovan Carroll more than fits the bill. As soon as their public display becomes a simmering private inferno, Rose backs off. Will Donovan be able to convince her that no revenge could ever be more satisfying than falling hopelessly and passionately in love?

THE ANDERSON FAMILY

Available January 2016!

"Readers will love Iris's tenacity and her resolve not to let anyone stop her from achieving her goals... The dialogue is strong and the characters are well-rounded." —*RT Book Reviews* on THE LOVE GAME

HARLEQUIN®
www.Harlequin.com

KPRH4350116

REQUEST YOUR FREE BOOKS!

2 FREE NOVELS PLUS 2 FREE GIFTS!

KIMANI™
ROMANCE

Love's ultimate destination!

THE WORLD IS BETTER WITH

Romance

Harlequin has everything from contemporary, passionate and heartwarming to suspenseful and inspirational stories.

Whatever your mood, we have a romance just for you!

Connect with us to find your next great read, special offers and more.

f /HarlequinBooks

🐦 @HarlequinBooks

www.HarlequinBlog.com

www.Harlequin.com/Newsletters

HARLEQUIN®

A *Romance* FOR EVERY MOOD™

www.Harlequin.com

April Knight crouched next to a young girl who sat with
a cello positioned between her spaced knees. The large,
slightly scarred instrument dwarfed her, but the teen
didn't seem intimidated. She looked on intently as, with
her signature calmness, April corrected whatever misstep
the girl had just made on the piece they were practicing.
She instructed her on how to glide the bow along the
taut strings. The result was fluid. A mesmerizing note
resonated throughout the space.

Once she was done assisting the room's lone cello
player, April returned to the front of the room. When
she turned and spotted him, her face lit up with a smile.
Several of the students—those who were not engrossed
in reading their sheet music—turned to see who had

captured their teacher's attention. April held up a hand and mouthed *five minutes*.

Damien nodded. Leaning a shoulder along the door-jamb, he folded his arms across his chest, crossed his ankles and studied the woman standing at the helm of the class. It had been months since he'd seen her, from the time when he had run into her at a Christmas party that one of his clients had invited him to at a loft in the Warehouse District. That had been what? Six months ago?

He'd arrived late, and April had been on her way out. Their encounter had been nothing more than a quick hug and profuse thanks from April for the donation Damien had given to A Fresh Start. They'd both promised each other that they would meet for coffee so they could catch up, but whenever he'd thought about calling her over the past six months something else had always come up.

Five minutes came and went, but Damien didn't dare interrupt April as she coached her pupils through a delicate piece. Besides, watching her in action was too entertaining to bring it to an end.

And to Damien's surprise he was watching her with more interest than he ever remembered watching his friend before. She wore soft yellow capri pants that hit just past her calves, a smart choice on this warm day. She probably had the heat and humidity in mind when she chose to pair it with the sleeveless white button-down blouse, but Damien thought it was the right choice for an entirely different reason.

Don't miss
PASSION'S SONG by Farrah Rochon,
available February 2016 wherever
Harlequin® Kimani Romance™ books and ebooks are sold.